CHASING THE DEVIL

Devil is dodging and diving?
I guarantee he's conniving!

M.J. Heywood

To our heavenly father without whom I would not have done any of this.
To my long-suffering husband Ron, for his love and patience.
To my friend Martin, for reading so many redrafts.

CONTENTS

ACKNOWLEDGEMENTS

A very special thanks to Marcus Barber who was
important in tying up my loose ends.
My thanks to Jim Lewis for early comments.
Thank you to everyone on the publishing team.

PRELUDE

Flies. Nefarious little buggers that swim around in front of your face; you swat them and they laugh at you, dipping and diving and heading straight back at you. When one leaves, another takes over. They land on your face, your legs, your hair, your arms, your food; they swim in your drinks and they eat your cakes. Sitting at the street café table, he was swinging his arms around like an octopus fighting for its life. The heat of the day was not helping. Flies, he pondered, leave behind their white squirmy babies who repeat the whole process again having reached maturity. He hated flies, but they reminded him of Cairo. Cairo, the home he longed to return to. He had been all around the world and he finally wanted to go home to sleep, for his soul to at last be in the home he missed, but the chase was on. There was one who knew how to end the pain that he was going through, but it appeared that every time he came close to seeing them, they would simply depart. But he always knew when they were close by, it was like having a sixth sense and he was certain he could smell something. It was difficult to explain the smell, but sulphur and rotting body was a close description. It could be weaponised if he ever put his mind to it. What he did know, though, was that when the smell was infiltrating his nose, there were absolutely no flies, none whatsoever; they obviously knew better than to hang around. Thutmose was sure he was the only one who could smell it and resolved to be more dedicated to his cause.

Thutmose picked up a toothpick from the container on the café table and stabbed the fly that was walking on it. He had got better at it over the millennia – quicker. He picked it up and twizzled it around, staring at the fly as it pulsed and squirmed on the wooden pick, rather like an hors d'oeuvre. "Serves you right, Ya Kha-ra," *('You shit' in Egyptian)* he said. He caught sight of a little boy at the next table staring at him, his curly brown hair blowing in the breeze, holding on to his mother's leg for security. Thutmose smiled broadly at him, then promptly ate the fly, opening his mouth as he chewed, so the child could see the whole slaughter as the fly was split and crushed by Thutmose's teeth. The child looked horrified and grabbed tighter to his mother's leg, looking back at Thutmose with wide eyes.

Thutmose stood up and picked up his jacket. He glanced towards the mother but she was looking the other way chatting to a friend, her arms in a lazy insecure hug around the child. Thutmose mouthed, "You're next," to the little boy, then turned away with an ugly smirk. He was not sure why he did it… Perhaps it was because he could. It was not the first time he had been cruel and uncaring; lately it seemed that he was getting more used to this side of his personality.

Thutmose's mother gave birth to him in the year c. 2613. It was said that she was visited by a god in the middle of the night and the next day when she awoke, she was pregnant. Thutmose's father was elderly and had not paid any attention to his young wife for many months; her pregnancy did nothing to improve their relationship. As she was going into labour, Thutmose's father had left for the evening and would not be back until early morning, visiting one of the bars in the town of Cairo to watch the young ladies dance and forget his sorrows at home. Giving birth alone, his mother had been shunned by her friends and villagers due to the miracle pregnancy. Gossip and rumours were rife. Thutmose's cries filled the house when he was born, as though he already had an idea of what was coming. His mother, exhausted and bleeding profusely, fell back onto her bed and slowly slipping into unconsciousness, passed away. Suddenly, absolute quietness descended, and Thutmose fell into a slumber. Through the silence, an angel passed through the wall of the house and walked to the bedside, looking sadly at the stillness of the woman's body. He walked to the window and shut his eyes. "What do you think? Shall we take the baby too, or just the mother?" Then he opened his eyes and the most beautiful pearlescent eyes smiled upwards towards the heavens. There was a small break in the clouds. "Amaya, time to go," he said. The spirit of Amaya rose and he bundled her up into his arms. She looked so tiny in the arms of this giant angel. She turned and looked at her child with a mixture of sorrow and happiness. "You will know him," Jophiel whispered and a second later, they were gone.

At Jophiel's departure, a foul stench filled the air in the small stone house. Out of the shadows emerged a hideous being, dragging a long bulbous tail behind him, but the closer it got to the window and the light of the moon, the more beautiful it became. It was surely, the most beautiful and perfect of any angel, with skin like porcelain and beautiful pearlescent eyes. Long flowing white hair, a body perfected by God himself, he shone brightly, so much so that his light could bring brightness to the world for miles around. Bit of a giveaway when he was trying to stay under the radar of his heavenly father, not that God needed it. He chased Lucifer around like Pac-Man.

Lucifer beamed an evil little smile and looked up towards the sky. "Oh, all is fair in the fight for souls, my brother." He snickered. The sarcasm dripped out of his voice like lava from a volcano. He turned his attention to the small bundle that was naked and lying on the blood-stained bed. Opening his mouth, a long, whispery, snakelike tongue skipped past the child's cheekbone, leaving a small scar he would carry always. Lucifer walked towards the baby and turning back into his hideous form, lingered by the child. "We will meet again," he sniggered, "and when we do… oh, what fun." Lucifer turned to go, then remembered something. Clicking his fingers in the air, he smirked. "Ooh, where are my manners?" He went back to Amaya's body and pulled her by her legs. The body made a thud and her head banged onto the floor. "Don't get up on my account, just pulling your legs." Lucifer laughed heartily at his own quip then disappeared back into the shadows.

Thutmose gave a little frown and his little hand touched his nose as though he had smelled something unpleasant, but his sleep was undisturbed. It would be one of the few nights he would sleep in complete peace. During the early hours of the morning a loud cry and yell sounded out down the streets. Amaya was buried quickly; bodies deteriorated quickly in the Cairo heat.

CHAPTER 1

Thutmose sauntered down a small side street and into a small, dark, dingy bar. He had been coming here every time he visited Italy over the last century. This building had fallen and been renovated many times over the millennia, and strangely enough, it always ended up serving alcohol to the public. He knew that his quarry had visited this vicinity whilst Caligula and Nero were in power. Less frequently when other Caesars were in power, and hardly at all during the time of Marcus Aurelius. The bar was frequented by all classes of people and had been for centuries, but they didn't come here for the women or the men or even the alcohol. They came because there was something quite magical about the place. In order to make you relaxed, the seats shifted and moulded to your body. If you were tired, the chairs would wrap around you and make you comfortable. Equally when it was time to leave, the seating would drop you onto the floor to wake you if you were sleeping and a loud gong sound would chime, and keep chiming until you left. During the day, the bar seemed to disappear into nothingness, only to re-emerge when the sun set, and it was only those of a preternatural state who could locate it. A member of the public had found it once by accident and it had not ended well. The Mind Mob had been despatched to make sure he forgot everything he saw and he spent the rest of his life mumbling about fairies and unicorns.

Thutmose had stumbled across it one evening, when he was almost into oblivion with drink. He remembered falling through the door and asking for a drink at the bar. He was supplied with coffee and suddenly felt like he did not want to argue about it. As the evening wore on, and a few coffees later accompanied by a hangover, he saw people get up and begin to dance to the sound of an accordion and folk flutes. The men playing the instruments were of a very large build – extraordinarily large. Thutmose had not seen this size of man since the fight between David and Goliath. They were very handsome, heavily set and appeared very strong. Their music filled the air and seemed to bring life to everything. Those asleep in chairs were pushed up by the seating to join in the dance. He felt a little shove from his chair and couldn't believe what he was feeling. The music made him want to tap his feet and dance. People began to sing and he wanted to sing. It felt ethereal and just for a moment, he forgot about Egypt and the reason he was searching. People tried to pull him into the dance, but he suddenly came to his senses, jumped up and disengaged himself. He lurched towards the door and fell into the street. The musicians turned to each other again and a slight flash of pale blue flickered in their eyes. They began to play their enchanting music again at the demanding chants of the crowd.

Thutmose didn't run because of the music or the dancing, he ran because of the stench, he ran because speed and time was of the essence to catch his target. He knew they were around this area, particularly in the winter. Thutmose, in his drunkenness had unknowingly been less than fifteen feet away from the Ergoges, an ethereal tribe who wander around Planet Earth, unbeknownst to the public, and they make sure things in the world happen at the right time and in the right place, at least they try to. They knew about Thutmose and they tried to get him out of the pub because he was in danger of missing the one he needed to speak to, but in all honesty, they rarely had luck with this particular individual themselves. But the target did not want to speak to Thutmose and went to great pains to avoid him. Thutmose was older now and knew the score. Moreover, when his target passed through the veil betwixt worlds, they only had ten to fifteen minutes to play with. Thutmose's target was chasing a witch who had cursed him using a reveal spell. This now meant that people knew almost immediately who he really was, hence the short period of time he had to enter through the veil. The element of surprise and suave sophistication in talking people into parting with their most prized asset, had effectively been removed. The witch was the only one who could remove the spell, but she was very elusive and had put a spell on herself which informed her when the individual was close. She knew all about the veils and knew how to work them to her advantage; she had effectively removed the shock factor. "What's the point of being all scary and all knowing if you don't know how to remove a witch's spell?" the target had whinged. "Come on, Fugly." His companion was called Fugly because… well… you can guess.

The next evening, having missed him yet again, Thutmose made his way towards the bar. He flung open the door and strode meaningfully towards the barman. Too late to duck, the barman had no option except to speak to him. Thutmose stared at the barman. "Well, has he been?"

The barman stared back at him. "I can't be sure," he said.

Thutmose sighed and tilted his head. "Are you sure?"

"Yes, sure I'm sure," said the barman.

"Well if you're sure, are you sure you're sure about being sure and you're sure?"

The barman said. "Well I'm sure that I'm sure, I'm sure?" He was now rubbing his chin.

"But are you sure, in your sureness, that you're sure about being sure and sure that you're sure? Because you did say that you can't be sure, so if you can't be sure, then how are you sure that you're sure about being sure when you can't be sure?"

The barman whimpered and a little bead of sweat dripped off his head. Thutmose noticed this and continued. "Because you see," he said, "it's very important to me, and if you are sure that you're sure, but aren't sure because you can't be sure…"

"STOP!" shouted the barman. "I'm not sure…" Thutmose was about to interrupt but the barman put up his hand to stop him and said, "but I am sure someone else will know the answer."

Thutmose stepped back from the bar. "OK then," he said, "but are you sure they will be sure?" The barman humphed, and moved away from Thutmose, walking to the rear of the building. Thutmose smiled, pushing his hands into his pockets.

"I'll be back shortly!" shouted the barman.

"Are you sure?" shouted Thutmose… A reply came and he couldn't make out what it was, but he was sure it was rather rude. Thutmose sat down and waited; he needed all the help he could get. The barman slipped through the veil; he had no intention of returning to the bar. He would advise that Thutmose was still searching.

CHAPTER 2

"It's beautiful. God will be really pleased with this gift and he will know how, why, when and who to give it to." The twelve angels all sighed. "It's taken us a thousand years to make it in complete secrecy, and imbue it with eternal power. Tiny elements of mankind, love, kindness, madness, passion, music, skills of all kinds, artistry and tiny elements of all of us, and the huge element of eternal life, all in one little package. How did we manage to keep it so secret?"

There was a short cough. "Erm… well, perhaps not so secret."

The eleven other angels turned and looked… Gabriel flushed bright red…

"Oh flipping heck, Gabriel," Uriel stormed. "Who have you told?"

"Well…?" they all chimed in. "Well?"

"I told Lucifer…"

"Oh, you so did not," said Ariel. "If I was Loki, my fiery sword…"

"Ariel…" shouted Michael, "That's not what we do…"

"No, we don't, that's my job," sulked Loki.

Michael turned to look at Gabriel. "Gabriel, what the flip…?"

"Flip is exactly where it's going to end up if we don't hide it," said Raphael.

"Why did you tell Lucifer, Gabriel?" Michael asked.

"Well…" she said, "it sort of came out in conversation when we were talking about his skateboard."

"Oh, wait a minute…" laughed Raphael. "Satan has a skateboard?"

Gabriel shrugged. "Well yes, he does… and he doesn't like being called Satan… it's the whole Satan, Santa, Satan… thing… and Nick, Old Nick, you know, it all relates to Christmas… His skateboard… was supposed to be a secret…" She drifted off.

"And you just aren't very good at keeping secrets, are you, Gabriel?"

"I was trying to share," she said. "You know, the whole sort of, helping your neighbour, the guy or girl who's down…"

Michael looked at her. "Gabriel, of all the fallen angels to have told, Lucifer was a huge mistake!" he yelled. "He doesn't have long and this would give him an extra one thousand years!"

"Lucifer was a literal mistake," said Jophiel.

"This could be really dangerous," said Michael.

"I'm sorry," Gabriel whimpered.

"So Satan has a skateboard, eh?" laughed Raziel. "I love it, I love it. A skateboard…"

"Please don't say anything, Raziel," she begged.

"You know me, I keep the secrets of God," said Raziel, "but that doesn't mean he won't find out you told us."

"We need a plan," said Raphael.

"Marvellous," said Jophiel. "We're archangels and what do we need? A plan. Well I tell you now, I don't need a plan, I need a drink."

They all tittered at the last time angels had a drink, but that's another story. It's true to say that alcohol is now banned in Heaven.

Michael stepped forward and said, "OK, give the Lapis Lazuli to me and I'll hide it."

"Why can't we give it to God now?" said Azrael.

"Because it's for his birthday and that's not for another 300 Earth years."

"But where are you going to hide it?" said Gabriel.

Michael looked at her incredulously. "Gabriel? Seriously?"

"Well, Heaven is an open book. He'll find it in seconds," she said. "He's got a nose like a Sneezehazer."

For the innocent, a Sneezehazer is a heavenly dog which can find fallen angels in a second. Their smell makes fallen angels sneeze and their fur makes things hazy so they can't see. However, as Lucifer was the first created by God, he is the only fallen angel they cannot find.

Michael frowned at Gabriel and all the angels turned and looked at her. Turning quickly and spinning on his heel, Michael ran two steps, jumped and flew high into the heavens before heading towards Earth. His speed was incredible… It was quite a sight to see. His wings spread out like a huge white cloud, every feather so perfect, glistening silver and gold; colours of every spectrum shot through each feather like they were dancing in their happiness that they were part of his wings. So downy, they looked soft enough to fall asleep on, but the strength of them was prominent too. Michael shone like a beacon of the world. His long fair hair flew behind him, each individual hair glistening in the sun with gold and silver, and his golden armour on his very perfect figure, shone in the brightness of his light. His porcelain features concentrated into his flight, his very beauty made God weep when he created him.

"He's beautiful," said Gabriel, in awe. "I could fall asleep on his wings."

The other angels cringed. "We were all bloody short changed," said Jophiel.

Michael landed gracefully on Earth in the desert outside Cairo. He changed his appearance immediately to take away attention from himself. He chose clothes that would help him to fit in with the crowds. He wore a knee-length shirt, with a kilt, a string of beads and bracelets. He looked quite the wealthy man. He lost his angelic face and showed instead a grey-haired, wrinkled, bearded man. He couldn't possibly bring attention to himself. Proud of his choice, he threw his shoulders back, concealed his magnificent wings, and began to walk out of the desert and towards the town of Cairo. He could fly a short distance, but he really couldn't risk it.

"Well, hello Mikey," said a voice, and right next to him appeared Lucifer.

"What do you want, Luci?" Michael said. "I'm busy right now."

Lucifer glanced at him. "Oh, I know you are, and I know what you have with you, and don't call me 'Luci'. Don't play the 'do I have it or not?' game, Mikey, we both know I was the pride and joy of Daddy before you were, and we can read each other's minds. I know you can try to block me, but knock-knock, Mikey, I'm coming in."

Michael stopped and looked at Lucifer. "Watching too many gangster films again, Luci? You really are a sad and pathetic little twit, aren't you? Now get lost before I turn you into a toad or something."

Lucifer laughed. "Angels don't do tricks, Michael, unless you are me, of course, so why not just hand it over and I'll be gone? You can always make another one in say… ooh, I don't know… a thousand years?"

Within a second Michael had Lucifer in a headlock. "Didn't see that coming, did you, Luci?"

Lucifer stamped on Michael's foot but he didn't let go. When angels battle, on principle, their powers against each other are not used no matter what, so Lucifer remained in human form and couldn't release himself as a puff of smoke or the dragon; he was always fair in a fight – that was about the only redeeming feature he had. Michael started to rub his knuckles on Lucifer's head.

"Luci, Luci, you're so pukey."

"Michael, stop it," Lucifer said, "or I swear to God…"

"Oh you will, will you?" said Michael. "Let's test that theory, shall we? I don't think he will listen to you anymore, you little toad."

They began to turn and spin in a circle that created a cyclone. Faster and faster they spun. Lucifer pulled his head free. "Ow, my ears!" he squealed, and the fight intensified. Hopping backwards and forwards towards each other, they slapped and pinched. Neither could emit light to blind the other in case they brought attention to themselves. On and on they fought and Michael began to wear Lucifer down. The ground began to shake, stone statues began to wobble, the sand swirled and spread, winds started to stir, cracks began to appear in the ground beneath them, heat began to rise, there were spits of fire showing in the cracks, when suddenly there was an almighty crack of thunder and the clouds opened. A voice which only they could hear, boomed down. "Michael, let Luci go right now!" Both stopped fighting immediately and nearly fell over because the ground became so still. Michael released his grip on Lucifer's hair and Lucifer fell to the sandy ground.

"My name is bloody Lucifer!" Lucifer yelled back.

Michael put his hands behind his back and looked up at the night sky. "Sorry, Father."

"What are you both doing? You nearly started an earthquake. That will NOT happen without my authority!" God was so furious that he created a rain storm that soaked both Lucifer and Michael. "Perhaps that will cool you down," he said. "I'm ashamed of you both, acting like children… 'Luci, Luci you're so pukey?' Michael, apologise right now, and why do you look so old? I've told you about burning the candle at both ends. You were so beautiful when I made you. What have you done? Never mind, I don't know what it is you're doing, but get it done and get back to what you should be doing, caring for mankind… or in Luci's case, causing problems for them to resolve."

"My name is bloody Lucifer," Lucifer yelled as he stood up, dusting off the sand. In his sulk, he turned into a demon.

"Michael!" shouted God.

"OK, Lucifer, I'm sorry you're pukey…"

"Michael!" God threatened.

"Oh, alright, I'm sorry I beat you… again… Well I did, Father."

"Are you both drunk? Because I remember last time…"

"No, no Father, we aren't drunk." Michael looked up through the rain. God sighed heavily and closed the clouds. The storm settled and Michael and Lucifer shook themselves dry.

"This isn't over, Mikey, and I'm right behind you," Lucifer said.

"Well you do stink…" Michael said, "so that's where you should be."

Lucifer was suddenly gone, but as he disappeared into the veil, his mind wasn't on revenge, it was on the Lapis Lazuli. How was he going to get his hands on it? It would help with his own problems and he just knew it would stop people finding out who he was. He could replace eternal life with something far more crushing, but he didn't have a thousand years to make one of his own. He knew his time was shortening with each passing year. He stepped onto his skateboard and shot off into the darkness. He had learned to handle it very well, spinning, jumping, sliding, bending over on it, doing handstands; it gave him great pleasure. "Well at least I have a skateboard and they don't." He smiled to himself and he disappeared into the darkness with his legs pointing upwards.

Michael wandered carefully around the city of Cairo. He liked mingling with humans; they were funny, and they lifted his spirits. He watched couples of all genders interacting with each other. How times were changing. He watched the humans shop, he watched them chatter, he watched them eat, he watched the joy and sadness that little things brought to them. He smiled at the joy and happiness they brought each other just by being together. He watched the insane playing of children, and then felt immediately embarrassed about his scuffle with Lucifer. He might apologise later. A voice in his head said, "That's my boy," and he saw the face of God smile.

After a while, he made his way out towards the desert again. Michael knew there was a very special place that the Lapis Lazuli could be hidden. He was going to hide it where he knew the pyramids were going to be built. He stood and sensed the area around him. It was vital that Lucifer was nowhere in the vicinity. Certain the area was clear of any otherworld entities, he closed his eyes and looked to the future and at the beauty of mankind. A dream of the future of Egypt flooded his mind. He lifted his hands up to the sky and slammed one down to the ground. It was done; it was so far beneath the earth that the little ringing sound and its light stopped completely. The energy was halted. No one, not even Lucifer, would find it here. It was buried within his vision and it was safe now until God's birthday. Three hundred Earth years would pass quickly in Heaven. He turned on his heel and ran. He ran faster and faster, enjoying the sensation of flight beginning to take over his body, then he jumped, and to make sure no one saw him, he became invisible and away into the heavens he soared.

CHAPTER 3

Despite his harsh upbringing, Thutmose had grown into a strong, handsome and academic young man. His long dark hair was plaited down his back, he wore only the finest cloaks, and today was a very special day. His years of studying mathematics would enable him to help design the resting chambers of the greatest Kings of Egypt. Today was so hot, he needed to make sure all the workers were sufficiently fed and given enough to drink for the huge job ahead. The foundations would need to be deep and the accuracy of the build would have to be correct to the finest millimetre. Any slight mistake and the whole thing could be out of sync and he would pay for it in more than money.

He worked closely with the greatest builder in Egypt, Snefru, his boss and mentor. The pyramids would be one of the greatest wonders of the world and the gods would bless Egypt with fertility and riches for eternity; at least that is what the Egyptians believed.

The day was becoming very hot and Thutmose told his men to take a break. He looked around and noticed that there was an indentation in the ground. Thutmose knew these indentations could mean that the ground was uneven and it could be detrimental to the building works. As everyone was resting, he mentioned it to Snefru. Snefru rubbed his chin. "I agree there could be a problem if we don't deal with it. We may need to make some changes and this won't go down well with Pharaoh. Check it out, Thutmose, see what you can find. I trust your knowledge and decision making. If you think there will be big issues, we will deal with them together." Snefru passed a flagon of water to Thutmose. Thutmose nearly finished a whole one for himself. Snefru laughed and slapped his back. "Hot days, my friend. Hot days." Thutmose walked back towards the uneven ground and put his foot inside it.

The earth gave way immediately and Thutmose fell into what appeared to be an extraordinarily deep hole, but was uninjured. Snefru turned around and realised that Thutmose had disappeared. He saw the hole in the ground and shouted for people to help; they ran towards the hole shouting Thutmose's name. "I'm down here!" he yelled out. Thutmose looked around to see what could have been the problem, but there didn't seem to be anything to worry about. *This is really strange,* Thutmose thought to himself. *If I've fallen into a hole, there must be something structurally wrong with this piece of ground. Is it an old well?*

Thutmose began to prod about inside the sandy hole. The ground seemed firm enough, so he knew he could get back out of the hole. Then he saw it. There was a small, dim, turquoise and white type of glow, but how could that be? It was under the sand, under the ground? He heard what he thought was a small tinkling sound and he was sure it was coming from the glow. Rather than being frightened, he was curious, as had always been his nature. He stuck his fingers into the sand and prodded about until he dug out the little blue glowing ball. *Wow, this is truly amazing,* he thought. *This might even make me rich. I wonder what it is.*

Thutmose heard voices above his head, and realised that

his crew were outside the hole and were dropping a rope into it. They shouted his name and he called back saying that he was well and uninjured. What was he going to do with the glowing ball? It had stopped ringing so he put it in his pocket.

Snefru shouted that they were stopping for the day, as the heat was too unbearable. They were making their way to Cairo and would spend the evening drinking and having fun. Did Thutmose want to come? He told them he would catch them up. The crew pulled him out of the hole and satisfied he was uninjured, they made their way towards Cairo. Thutmose said he would return home to clean up and meet them there. Muggings had increased with the influx of workers and the growing village around the pyramids so Thutmose decided to swallow the glowing ball and then regurgitate it at home where he would inspect it more closely. However, as the ball went down his oesophagus, he began to feel very unwell.

There was a shake and a vibrating sensation; he felt it in every part of his wings. Michael stopped and stood very, very still. It had been found, and he saw the face of the person who had found it. "Oh no, oh no, no, no," he said.

Jophiel looked at him… "Michael?"

Michael looked at Jophiel, then ran and flew. In a nanosecond Jophiel saw what Michael had seen. "Oh no." The picture flashed in his mind. "Hell," said Jophiel. "I knew this would happen."

"This could get really messy," said Ariel.

The angels gathered together and watched intently through the clouds.

Michael reached the spot where Thutmose was, but he was too late. He could do nothing. Thutmose was passed out on the floor. If he removed the energy now it would do two things. One, it would kill the physical human side of him, and two, he would turn into a demon. Given who Thutmose was, Michael could not risk anything. Of all the people in all the world who could possibly have found it, and by accident. There were preparations that needed to be done first. Possessing something as big as this all at once could also potentially be fatal. Michael needed to move him. He withdrew his wings and changed his appearance before anyone saw him. He looked around and saw that the opening to the largest pyramid was still open. As luck would have it, Thutmose had passed out in a spot unnoticed by other humans. Perhaps they thought the flash was lightning. He picked Thutmose up and made his way towards the pyramid. It was evening and people were either sleeping or talking in groups. Some turned and looked at this strange sight, a very large man carrying their manager. Michael needed to think fast. "Drunk," he shouted and rolled his eyes. People seemed to accept this and they went back to what they were doing.

As Michael made his way towards the pyramid, in a corner, out of sight and hidden by the darkness, there stood a figure. Lucifer watched balefully, but would remain unnoticed because he had wished it so. His long slimy tail slid back under his cloak; he pulled his hood further over his face and watched the spectacle. He would wait until they were inside the pyramid and then make a move. Why was Michael here and why had he come down personally? There was something amiss and Lucifer was going to find out what it was. This was definitely a very strange situation.

Michael took Thutmose inside the large pyramid and laid him

on the floor. Once inside, he reverted to his angelic form and stretched his wings. Wings get very cramped when hidden. "Thutmose, wake up," he said, and just as he was about to pass his hand over his face, he heard a noise.

"Hello, Mikey," said Lucifer.

Michael stood up. "You can't have him, Lucifer."

"Oh, come on now." He snickered. "He was going to be mine at some point anyway."

"I said no," Michael snapped, "and I *will* fight you, Lucifer."

Lucifer stepped forward, his yellow eyes burning and his pupils became slits. His face became the reptilian snake he had used before in the garden of Eden and he wisped his tongue out towards Michael.

"You've corrupted enough, and I will not let you take your son," said Michael. "It is not his fault he was born to you, but I can prevent you from taking him now."

Lucifer folded his arms and stepped further forward. As the candles in the pyramid began to glow brighter due to Lucifer's presence, he changed his appearance to that of the angel he once was. Always beautiful, his face had become as hard as stone. He did not flinch at anything Michael said.

"He is my seed, Michael. Man born of the..." He paused... He hated the word. "Devil... would walk the earth and... Well, you know the rest, I don't need to tell you. Why are you here though, Mikey? It is his 30th birthday and I'm sure you didn't come here to celebrate it with him. Now just step out of the way and we'll be gone. Is he drunk?"

Michael rolled his eyes. "No, he isn't drunk." Lucifer bent forward as if to pick Thutmose up. Michael put his hand on the hilt of his sword. "I said no, Lucifer..."

Lucifer's eyes flashed red and then they both stopped… Thutmose moved. "Oh… by the messengers of Sekhmet," he said.

"Not quite," said Lucifer, "but close enough…"

Michael took his hand away from his sword and reached for Thutmose. He pulled him up to his feet and on standing erect, Thutmose promptly vomited all over Michael's chest plate. "Like father, like son," tittered Lucifer. Now that was funny because Lucifer had in fact vomited on Michael at a Christmas party. Yes, angels celebrate too – no longer in Heaven by order of God, but that's another story.

Thutmose fell down again and Michael pulled him back up. Thutmose began to stagger around and kept falling. "What's wrong with me?"

"You've had too much to drink," said Michael.

Michael needed to play for time; he needed time to think of how to reverse this without damage, if there was a way, and he needed to keep Lucifer out of his head but he felt a pressing nudge.

"Knock, knock, Mikey…" laughed Lucifer.

Michael needed to concentrate on Thutmose. "You'll be fine in the morning, just keep looking into my eyes." Thutmose tried, but was sick again. "Thutmose!" shouted Michael. The roar of the angel made Thutmose turn. He looked at Michael, then he passed out again. "Oh, flip," said Michael.

"I'll take him off your hands…" said Lucifer.

Michael ignored Lucifer and bent over Thutmose. He put his hand to his head and he could feel the energy. The energy of 1,000 years was taking root; it was pulsating and he felt the buzz of electricity moving through Thutmose. His body began to tremble and his veins started to throb. They looked like they would burst through his skin. This was a very dangerous moment. Thutmose's eyes opened and closed, the pupils growing bigger and smaller, changing colour; the whites of his eyes looked like a deep purple. Vomit began to dribble out of Thutmose's mouth and down into his hair. He began to shake and his temperature was dropping. He appeared to stop breathing and suddenly Thutmose became ice cold. Michael dropped his head. It was too late. It was complete.

Lucifer, who had been watching this fascinating incident whilst sitting on the edge of a sarcophagus, suddenly shot up straight, realisation making his eyes widen. "Oh no, oh no. This is priceless." Lucifer laughed out loud and clapped his hands. "This is too good to be true. You've done it, haven't you? You tried to keep it from me and now, you have given it to my son! Of all the people in all the world." Lucifer threw his arms out and began to dance around and twirl, spinning himself up towards the ceiling and turning up the sand in the pyramid.

"It was not done purposefully," said Michael. "He stumbled across it. Please, Lucifer, you know the consequences of this action. You have to help me."

Lucifer stopped mid-air and shot down faster than the human eye could see. He was next to Michael. "Help you? Help you?" he spat. "You took centre stage from me, Michael. I was the chosen one and you threw me from my father's home. It was my rightful place and you destroyed everything. I loved you eternally, Michael, and had I ruled, I would have made you powerful, Michael, but look at you now, on your knees begging me. You are the same as any mortal on this planet. They all beg me, Michael, they all want fortune, success and a grandiose life, but I always win." He paused. "Oh yes, Michael, I always win. Everyone has to pay the piper, or should I say viper. Why would I help you when you helped to destroy me? You stopped loving me, and although you have something I want, I'm not begging or asking, Michael, I'm taking him. He's mine."

"Please… do not let us get into that old story again," said Michael. "He needs help, we need to deal with this, he could die."

Lucifer shifted shape. He became a demon so ugly and putrid that even Michael could hardly bear to look. "No," he growled. "He will be mine, Michael, and the world will know misery and sorrow like never before, and you have caused it." He stood back up, shifting back to an angelic form. Arrogantly, he said, "I'll be back for him in the morning." Waving his hand in the air and bowing sarcastically, Lucifer was gone.

Michael turned back to Thutmose. He vowed that he would try to make this right. He would keep Thutmose on the right track, whatever it took. He knew he had to tell God what had happened. God could correct this; he was sure he would understand when he told him the gift had been for him. He felt the sorrow of his companion angels in the sky; they were looking down on him. Michael would sit down and wait until dawn. Thutmose would need to know what had happened and the consequences of it… if he survived. Michael folded his wings around himself and watched. Angels never sleep.

The night wore on and Michael heard a sound. He felt a strange vibration and knew instantly it was Geb. He looked up. "Hello, Michael," smiled Geb.

Michael smiled. "Hello, Geb. It's wonderful to see you. How's Nut?"

"Pregnant," said Geb. "But I think your problem is bigger. I think, though, that both our problems could be over by morning, one way or the other," laughed Geb.

"My problem, hmmm, do you think you have a solution?" Michael was hopeful.

"Yes, kill him and I'll trap him in my body. Providing you don't do too much damage to his body, we can always put him back again without the energy. We can both extract it."

Michael looked at Geb with a frown. "Are you joking?"

Geb smiled. "No, I'm not. You can put his body in the earth and I'll do the rest. Just don't do the burning thing, we all know how that ends up."

Michael looked slightly disturbed. "I can't," said Michael. "Only God can kill a mortal."

"Well if you use your shield, he won't know," said Geb, "and our lad here is no longer a mortal, just remove the heart or the head."

"God knows everything," said Michael. "The shield is for me to use responsibly. If I used it for something like this, he would be very angry."

Geb put his head on one side and looked at the angel. "Michael, I think you're pretty much in the shit anyway," said Geb. "I know from the smell Lucifer has been here, but I can't work out why."

"I can't tell you," said Michael.

Geb bent down and prodded Thutmose. "He's hard," he said, "...and I know how uncomfortable that can be," Geb laughed. "What's that mark on his face? Was he burned?"

"No," said Michael. "He was bitten by a snake when he was a baby."

"Quite," said Geb. "So, what's your plan?"

"Why does everyone ask me what my flipping plan is?" Michael said. "If I had a plan that worked, none of this would have happened."

"Michael, just let me take him," said Geb, resigned. "I promise I'll bring him back in one piece. Our secret."

"No," said Michael, "it's not safe."

Geb looked out of a hole in the side of the pyramid. "Sun is rising, Michael. I have to go. If you change your mind…"

"I won't," he said, "but thanks."

Geb walked outside of the pyramid.

"Well?" said Lucifer…

"Nope, wouldn't go for it," said Geb. "Have to go, wife is about to give birth. WOW! Nice skateboard, Luci."

"Piss off, Geb," said Lucifer.

Michael felt disturbed by the conversation with Geb. *How did he know about the energy? Was it possible? No, he wouldn't.* He dismissed the thought from his mind.

As the sun began to rise and he heard the first sounds of humans moving around outside, Michael knew they would soon enter the pyramid. They couldn't find him here, or Thutmose.

The sound was getting closer. He closed his eyes and raised his hand and Michael and Thutmose were transported outside of the pyramid and a mile away into the desert. Michael bent down and put his hand on Thutmose's head. He would be awake soon. He had survived the night. His body was returning to normal and now he just looked like he was asleep. Michael looked into the sky and cast a shield; he could not allow God to see him just yet. The shield was a gift God had given to Michael alone; the gift of privacy. He was the only angel allowed such a privilege.

"I can't see him, he's gone," said Jophiel.

"No, he's still there." Metatron gave Jophiel a resounding slap on the back. "We need to go, and go now." The angels all took to flight and created a thunderstorm to cover them. The flashes of lightning would hide their wings in the brightness of the sky.

The sun was getting higher and a sandstorm began. Lucifer was on his way. Michael stood steadfast with his hand on the hilt of his sword. He looked down at Thutmose who remained still. Through the swirling red-hot sand, Lucifer came. He was in angelic form and wore his breastplate. Clearly, he was ready for battle. "OK, Mikey, hand him over."

Michael said nothing and continued to stare ahead at Lucifer. There seemed to be a darkness behind Lucifer that Michael had not seen before.

"You can't possibly win this, Mikey, now hand him over. He belongs to me… my seed… blah, blah, blah."

"I have not changed my mind, Lucifer; he will come with me. He still has his soul and I absolutely will not let you corrupt him." Michael steeled himself and stayed steadfast.

"Absolutely will not?" mimicked Lucifer in Michael's voice. Lucifer sighed. "Give him to me or you will suffer the consequences."

The sand began to thin and Michael saw that the darkness was in fact a swarm of dwarf demons behind Lucifer. "Felt the need to bring the family for protection, eh Luci?"

Lucifer peeled back his lips in a threatening growl, his face became ugly and he ran at speed towards Michael. Using all the angelic power and strength he had, Lucifer pushed Michael so hard it knocked him off his feet and sent him reeling. Michael corrected his body mid-air and landed upright, laughing. He ran towards Lucifer and their wings expanded. They flew back at each other and battle commenced. They pulled and twisted, swinging at each other with swords. They slashed at each other, trying to cut each other's wings off. As fast as they spun, the sand swirled with them. Neither was holding anything back and it became more violent.

Morning moved into midday and still they battled. The sun began to get blazing hot, the sand burned their feet, and this time neither gave any ground. It was dangerous for both of them, but ever the victor, it was clear that Michael was the stronger of the two and suddenly without warning, Lucifer changed.

It broke every rule in the book, but the dragon emerged. The head reared back and the spines shot upwards. Made of steel, they would be lethal. Huge wings flapped, turning up the sand, blocking out the sun. Dark shadows crawled around like large cockroaches. Claws outstretched, glistening with fire, there was a deafening roar and Lucifer sped towards Michael. In a split second Michael had moved and was on Lucifer's back. The dragon head moved left and right, lashing out with an acid tongue, trying to get Michael off his back. He spat fire and bits bounced off his spines, leaving no mark. Michael flew high with a shot of fire following him. He came down at speed and landed by Lucifer's left ear, driving his sword into Lucifer's neck, and the dragon suddenly retreated. Lucifer fell to the ground holding his neck.

"You know better, Lucifer," Michael chastised.

Lucifer rose again and flew towards Michael, stopping

within inches of his face. "You are foolish, my brother," he spat back. "You don't know who you are fighting. I was merely a deterrent. If you care to look, my son has gone. Of course, I didn't come alone." In a moment, Lucifer was gone; there was nothing except his laugh ringing in the air, almost a mockery to the Lapis.

Michael froze. What would he tell God now? He had effectively given Thutmose over to Lucifer; he had given Lucifer the extra 1,000 years he was looking for. His pride had made him think he could handle everything alone. The world would indeed go to Hell. Armageddon would arrive much sooner than planned.

"Do not worry," a familiar voice said. He turned and saw Metatron who smiled broadly. "We'll get him back. We were all engaged in fighting and some of the little runts took him. Sorry, Michael. Whilst you were fighting with Lucifer, I blinded those he brought with him, but the little cockroaches appeared from everywhere." Michael was devastated and rested on his knee, then Metatron frowned. "Michael, God will speak with you. He is very angry; I haven't seen him like this since Lucifer. You have a lot of explaining to do but you will not do it alone, we will come with you."

The angels all rose back into the heavens. God was all around them when they came into his presence, but he was very quiet.

The angels stood silently waiting for the voice of God. Their nervousness was palpable. Suddenly, the quiet was shattered by the music of a thousand organs playing '*I Am The One And Only*' (seriously, people, where did you think that song came from?) and a beautiful golden shaft of light appeared. The organ music got louder and louder and was almost deafening, even to the angels. Then it began to snow. The air around them became so cold, they began to grow icicles on their feathers. "Hells bells," said Ariel, at the risk of causing trouble by using those very words. "Why can't he just make a normal entrance instead of this bells and whistles stuff? Why can't we just have a meeting and sit around discussing problems? Or even a meeting room to discuss them in?"

The snow receded, then it rained, heavily. The angels were soaked. They stood around looking at each other, wiping rain off their noses, tutting and shaking the rain off their sandals. The rain created by God could cause angels' feathers to be soaked to the point that they were unable to fly. "Why does he do this?" asked Zadkiel, then suddenly everything stopped, and the air around them returned to normal.

Quietness descended again and the Lord God in Heaven appeared to the song of Cherubs. "Because, Ariel," he began, "nothing ever gets solved in meetings. We would need a meeting to discuss the meeting we just had. Have you really learned nothing from the human race? And Zadkiel, I do what I do, because I can. I am, the one and only," he said with a little laugh. No one answered because God wouldn't listen anyway. He was always right, and truly, he really was always right.

God was twice the size of the angels today and stood over them, looking down. He frowned. "Michael, you've broken rules and you have created, almost, Hell on Earth. As it happens, I know exactly what, how, where and why this came about. I now need to decide what to do about Thutmose. This also means, I may have to stop time. I have told you all that this was never a good thing; it rocks the universe and puts planets out of balance; it takes me months to put them right again. Your arrogance let you down in that fight, Michael. You should have walked away, but ever the warrior—"

"Father—" Michael interrupted. One look from God and Michael was silent.

"I will not enter Hell, Michael, unnecessarily, and I cannot make Lucifer give Thutmose back. You were all involved, I know, you all fought, but none of you thought for a minute that Lucifer would have a plan. After all the gifts I gave you… you chose to fight, and what is worse, you chose to fight because you wanted to. Did you think you were in a bar brawl?"

Jophiel put his hand up.

"I don't need answers, Jophiel."

Jophiel put his hand down.

"There could have been a much different ending to this. You used your shield to block me, Michael. What you should have done was bring Thutmose to me and I could have taken all that energy out. I am removing your privilege, Michael, and it will be up to you to earn it back. Why have you done this, Michael? Speak."

Of course, God didn't need to hear it from Michael, because he knew everything, but he always found it interesting to watch the angels and curiously observe if over the millennia, they had learned anything from him. God looked thoughtful. Lucifer had taken everything in and learned very quickly. In doing so, he thought he could overthrow God. That was one battle that would never be forgotten. Now, here was Michael. Arrogance had been Lucifer's downfall. He waited.

Michael knelt on one knee. "Father, we love you. We know that you created the universe and the world and all the things in it. We wanted to give you a present for your birthday. It was for you to pass to whomever you thought fit to receive it. I did not mean for Thutmose to find it. I was trying to hide it and I thought I had hidden it well. Father, the energy we created was for a thousand years of extra life. There were bits of all of us in it, bits we wanted to give back to you – joy, happiness, laughter, fun, smiles, hugs… Because you gave us these things from love, we wanted to give them back to you to pass to someone you saw fit, someone who would be chosen to be a saint. I'm sorry, Father. I will take whatever punishment you see fit for me."

Metatron stepped forward. "Father, please do not judge Michael too harshly. We were all guilty of getting involved in the energy production. None of us could foresee that Thutmose would find it."

God looked at Metatron. "But that is not true, is it, my son? You were all given the gift of prophecy and foresight. Are you now all becoming liars? Have you forgotten how I feel about liars?"

Metatron continued, "Father, in our excitement in developing this—"

God held up his hand and there was that awful sigh. "Wait," he said. "I will be back." He turned away and the organ sounded… Ariel went to say something and God shouted back, "Shut up, Ariel. *This is my moment, this is my perfect moment.*" Then he laughed again. "I think I've earned it, don't you?" Ariel stepped forward.

"Shut up, Ariel," said Chamuel. "We're in it deep enough already."

"I was just going to say I liked his taste in music," said Ariel.

After what seemed an eternity, and probably was, God returned. He was the same size as the angels now, which meant his anger had subsided, and he walked brusquely down a golden corridor which he created with *a few of his favourite things* as he walked. It was magnificent. "Impressive," said Metatron.

God smiled. He clapped his hands. "Right, I have decided the following. Michael, you will go to Hell."

Michael was horrified. "Father, please…"

"Let me finish," God said. There was a pause. "You will go to Hell and you will retrieve Thutmose. I will not give you any help whatsoever. You thought you could deal with the problem yourself, and you failed. Metatron, Jophiel, Ariel and Raguel will go with you. When you arrive, you will no doubt get into fights. My advice is to not let any of the dwarf beings bite you."

"Why?" said Ariel. "Will it change us into one of them?"

"No, but they cause nasty injuries," said God. "When you are in Hell, you will request Lucifer return Thutmose. What seems like a few hours to a mere human will actually have been hundreds of years. Thutmose could be anywhere and anybody by now. He may wish to remain with Lucifer, and it is going to be up to you to convince him otherwise. If you can't, I will have to deal with him myself and that's another battle we do not want. I am now trusting that you will all sort this out together. My last piece of advice is: be careful. There are many deceits in Hell and despite Lucifer being your brother, he is the King of Deceit. Your gifts will be useless in Hell, you may as well be mortal, you will need to use your mind and your intelligence. There is no place for bravado in Hell. Lucifer is the ruler and he will be lethal. Your brothers who are staying behind, will fill in for you and will go about their usual business. That is why I have split you into two groups. The unemployed angels will help to fill in for you whilst you are gone. Should you succeed, you will bring Thutmose to me and we will discuss his reintegration back into the human race." God turned his back, and in a nanosecond, was gone.

The angels took to the skies where Michael flew at the forefront at speed. His brightness lit the way for the other angels to follow. They began to descend and as they hit the ground, they felt warm air. They were on the outskirts of Hell.

The veil between worlds split and in front of them emerged a dead and barren landscape. The trees were black, the ground hard, black and grey. Ice formed but quickly melted only to ice over again. No flowers, no grass, just black trees that looked like they had burned for a thousand years.

"What a soulless place," murmured Raguel.

"Not quite." Michael looked at Raguel. "This is the home of the souls of the dead."

There was a foul smell and subdued screams. "Where's the fire?"

"Shut up, Joph." Michael was listening; he could feel a slight vibration beneath his feet.

"What is that?" Ariel looked down.

"It's a pointer as to where we will find the entrance to Hell," said Michael.

"So, we're not there yet?" said Raguel.

"Oh, we're here alright, but Lucifer moves the entrance so you have to look for it."

They walked on and it began to get warmer. A pathway appeared made of burning hot coals. "Keep walking." Michael looked ahead. "Take no notice of the coal."

"Ooh, I'm firewalking!" laughed Ariel.

"That will never catch on," said Metatron.

As they walked, it became hotter but it did not affect them. Ariel was dusting off ash and tutting. Michael saw Lucifer approaching. Lucifer looked so beautiful. His long, blond, fair hair, full of waves and curls, flowed over his shoulders. His brightness shone to outshine that of Michael. He had the physique of a god and his battle uniform was spotless. His high chiselled cheekbones structured a face only God himself could have created. His beautiful mother of pearl eyes smiled and his wings were stretched huge and like Michael's, glistened white, shot through with the colours of the rainbow. The fire around him could not touch him.

"Bloody hell," said Jophiel, "he's absolutely the most beautiful and finest of angels I have ever seen. Sorry, Michael, but he's gorgeous."

Metatron winced. Michael felt a twinge of jealousy and then disconnected from it. Hell provoked all sorts of emotions and exposed them, but Michael's twinge of jealousy was a falsity created in Hell. Jophiel was right, though; Lucifer really was beautiful. Michael remembered why he had loved his brother so much. God had certainly created a god.

Lucifer put his arms around Michael. "Hello, Mikey. Missed me, eh? Knew you wouldn't be able to stay away from me."

Raguel moved forward. "We're here for Thutmose, Lucifer, now hand him over."

Suddenly Lucifer's eyes flashed red, then he smiled and his

face was back to angelic. "He isn't here. It has been 400 years, Michael. Did you think, as a human given the power of choice, he was going to remain here? He wanted to go back to Earth. He was confused, upset, scared and he simply didn't like the smell. He stayed for 200 years then he went."

"You're lying," said Raguel.

"No, I'm really not. He wanted to leave and leave he did."

Michael looked into Lucifer's eyes. "How?"

"What?"

"How did he leave? He's a human with an immortal soul. How did he leave here without your help?"

"I took him back."

"You're lying."

"I took him back," spat Lucifer.

Michael pushed past Lucifer and the angels followed. Lucifer was gone.

"Keep walking!" shouted Michael, and they marched on ahead.

They walked past cities that resembled cities on Earth. London, Moscow, New York, and in Hell, all of them were burning. The closer they got to the heart of Hell, the worse it became. They heard screams and saw people crying and begging at the roadside. They couldn't do anything for them; this was Lucifer's domain.

"He's here," they all said in unison. It was the energy that they felt. Just as they were getting closer to Lucifer's kingdom, they stopped. There was a table laid out with games and food.

Ariel's stomach churned. "I'm hungry."

"It's a trick," said Metatron. "You're an angel, you don't get hungry. Don't touch it. It could be dangerous."

As they passed the table, Ariel picked up a pear. Metatron turned around. "Put it back, Ariel."

Ariel laid the pear back on the table, so it seemed, and as they walked on Ariel bit the pear. All the angels turned and looked at him. "Oh, Ariel, you total fool."

Ariel now had the head of a pig. "Oh, poo," he said.

They slowly approached Thutmose. But Michael noticed that he didn't seem to be aware of his surroundings. He was walking around and taking measurements, he was writing things down. He was talking to people, at least he thought he was, and was pointing to things that were not there. "Great," said Ariel, "he's gone mad." The angels continued to watch him.

"No, there's a lot more to this," said Metatron. "He hasn't the faintest idea where he is. He thinks he's on Earth. I'm sure of it. What is this?"

"Smart, is what it is," said a voice. Lucifer stood with his arms folded. Gone was his beautiful angelic perfection. They were talking to a horned god. "When I brought him here, he could easily have died of shock. You don't just take someone from Earth and then awaken them in Hell, or Heaven, Michael." His eyes were like steel. His features exaggerated; sunken eyes looked sarcastically at the angels. "He thinks he is still working on the pyramids. Mathematically he is a genius, but of course his genius, and his devastatingly good looks, come from me. I'm keeping him until its time, then *schloop*," Lucifer made the sound of a vacuum, "hello Armageddon."

He walked by the angels and stroked Michael under his chin with his long, bony fingernail. Michael stepped back.

"So, you have come to take him away, have you? Your

gifts are useless here and I can effectively keep him here for eternity. Your only challenge is to try to get by me, convince him to go with you and then leave in one piece. Are you up to it?"

Raguel stepped forward with his hand on his sword.

"Oh, give it a rest, Raguel," yawned Lucifer. "You'd be wingless in seconds."

Michael put his hand on Raguel's arm. "It's fine, brother, we will discuss this like the divine beings of example we are." Michael looked towards Lucifer. "Lucifer, we can discuss this with you, but not in this form. Please talk to us as we were many eons ago, brother to brother, angel to angel."

Lucifer's heart ached for Michael. He wanted to speak with him, to play fight with their swords as they had before the change, but his anger at what had happened prevailed. There was no forgiveness. Lucifer quickly looked the other way so Michael could not see the stirring of mixed emotions in his eyes. Composing himself, he turned back. "If you want to talk to me, Michael, you will accept me for who I am, in my kingdom." His voice began to rise. "I am king here, not you."

Michael sat down. "Then, my king, let us sit down and talk."

As they did so, Lucifer noticed Ariel and grinned. Ariel grunted. "Don't worry, Ariel, you will change back to your less-than-average self when you leave," laughed Lucifer. "Unless I roast you on a spit first. I quite like pork."

Lucifer manifested a huge court and he was sat at the high table wearing the clothes of a judge. His minions surrounded the court and the other fallen angels appeared as spectres, their sorrow leaking into the courtroom. Lucifer looked directly at Michael. "Now begin."

"Lucifer, I know that Thutmose is your son and I know you wanted him to know you. He is, though, trapped in time; you have stopped him moving forward and he will not progress."

Lucifer tilted his head and looked at Michael.

Michael continued. "He needs to live a normal life. He deserves that much given how much his father struggled to bring him up, and he fought to be in the position he is today. You have to let him come back with me. We could change time, put him back where he was and make sure he doesn't find the stone. Please?"

Lucifer looked at Michael. "No. Are we done now?"

"Lucifer, you said you would discuss it," said Michael.

"We are discussing it, Michael, and I said no, end of discussion. Best if you leave now, I feel, otherwise Thutmose will have company."

"Don't be so selfish," said Michael.

Lucifer stood up. "Michael." Metatron touched his arm. "That wasn't wise."

Lucifer walked towards Michael. "I said leave," he hissed. "This is my final warning." He began to breathe heavily and a transformation started to take place.

"Lucifer, stop," pleaded Michael. "I'm sorry, I truly am. Please?"

Lucifer turned and pulled his bulbous, ugly, snakelike body back to his chair. The big, snakelike, swollen tail came to rest on the steps. "You see this before you, Michael? Thutmose is the only thing that reminds me that once I was beautiful. Can you see my beauty in him, Michael? My beauty now illusory, just like the world above. Just like the humans see it. If they saw the real world, they would want to die. If I send him back now, I will lose him. He will never know me and if you remove the energy, he will live a mortal life of only a few years. He will die and his soul will go to…" he paused… "him." He shoved his finger upwards. "He will never be mine again. I cannot allow that to happen. I need him to know me. I need him to discover who I truly am, and he may even accept me."

Michael saw a vision; it flashed between him and Lucifer – they had always had a connection. The truth was, Lucifer was planning to take the energy out of Thutmose and he would work for Lucifer as a demon. Lucifer knew the dangers, but he was only interested in the thousand extra years he would gain, and he would be transformed into the handsome angel he was for those thousand years. He knew his time was shortening. Lucifer seemed oblivious to the fact that Michael had seen the deceit. But Michael also remembered what God had said; there were many deceits in Hell and Lucifer was the King of Deceit. He could not be sure that Lucifer was unaware.

Use your mind and intelligence, God had said. Michael looked at the other angels who were looking to him for some sort of sign. He cleared his mind and opened it so that Lucifer could gain access. He could gain access anyway in Hell, but this would make it easier and less painful. Michael would appeal to Lucifer's vanity, and with any luck, the other angels would follow his lead.

"Lucifer, you are and always have been beautiful. It is your anger and rage which keeps you from the being you truly are. Keeping Thutmose here is not the real you. Mankind turned you into the bogey man under the bed to scare children into being good." Lucifer looked at Michael and said nothing. Michael continued, "Thutmose thinks he is creating something, but in fact he is creating nothing. You would not want a son who bent to your every wish and created things that were shadows and dust. You would want a son to be proud of, surely? Think of the things he can achieve in the time he has on Earth. You yourself could help him whilst he is there and when his time comes, you would be able to say that you had helped him and he would have a valid choice as to where he wanted to be. Give him that chance, Lucifer."

The other angels sat and listened and Michael looked at each one of them as he spoke before finally returning his gaze to Lucifer. Raguel gave a nod. "I would like to help if you would let me, Lucifer. Do you want him to be able to fight like the king you are? I could help with that."

Metatron stood up. "Already a mathematical genius, he would excel, and physics. No one would be able to touch his building work; it would be fine, striking and totally ingenious."

Jophiel said, "Strength and positivity."

Ariel stood up, his huge pig head proudly pointing upwards. "And when it is time to leave the earth, I will be there to help you to help him make the decision in your favour. I will be there with him, watching over him, when you have to be somewhere else."

Lucifer looked at the angels. "You would do this for me? The forsaken son of God himself? You would guide my son through his life?"

Michael opened his mind further and almost dragged Lucifer into it. Lucifer turned into his angelic self, though his wings were slightly darker.

"Lucifer, you've got a bit of… on your… sort of on your wing ends…" said Jophiel.

"Yes, it's the smut from the fire," said Lucifer thoughtfully.

Lucifer stood and stared at Thutmose and walked to him. Thutmose couldn't see him. If he did, he would probably die on the spot. People did that when they saw the Devil, it was really embarrassing, as if the smell wasn't bad enough. Lucifer knew the angels were right. "Sleep," he said, and Thutmose slept. "What is Father going to do?" Lucifer bent his head and slightly tilted it to listen to Michael.

"Stop time," said Michael. "He'll correct everything. He'll put the world back to the restore point."

Lucifer wanted to rage and yell and strike these angels down; his jealousy was all consuming. He wanted to watch them burn over a pit. The beautiful beings that God had sent to mock him. He wanted to go back with them. He wanted what they had, but in his heart, he knew he wanted more. He couldn't really go back. He would still try to unseat God. There had been a war in Heaven before and he had lost. He just needed extra time. Now they were taking his son. Lucifer trusted Michael. He didn't know why, he just did. He handed Thutmose over. He looked so small and childlike in their arms. He looked into Michael's eyes. "Take care of him, Michael." Michael nodded and they began to walk out of Hell and back to the entrance ready to return home.

"That was too easy," said Metatron.

Michael glanced. "Just keep walking," he said.

They were desperate to fly, but their wings were useless where Lucifer reigned. They thought they saw something in the rocks as they were making their way out; it looked like large, dark bouncing balls.

"We're being followed," said Jophiel. "Lucifer was lying. He doesn't want us to leave, does he?"

"No," said Michael. "Pick up the pace." They began to

almost trot. It was a good job Thutmose was human and not another angel.

Suddenly Ariel let out a wild, long scream. One of Lucifer's dwarves had attacked. It had sunk its teeth into Ariel's wing and it began to bleed quite badly. "Run!" shouted Raguel.

They started running and the earth beneath them began to crack. Fire, brimstone, lightning, and rain all began to swirl and swirl around them. They were nearing the opening to the outside but their wings were useless. They kept running. The dwarves were everywhere and even though they were slicing them with their swords, they split into two with one swipe, and three with two swipes. The more they sliced them, the more they split up. Just as they were reaching the opening to outside, Lucifer flew into view. He was three times as large when he was angry. He flew down to block their way. Michael threw Thutmose to Metatron, who was ahead of him. Metatron threw Thutmose to Raguel, who threw him to Jophiel, who threw him back to Michael. Lucifer's eyes were darting all over but he could not be certain who would catch Thutmose next. The angels reached the opening and jumped, their wings spreading, and they flew.

Metatron had caught hold of Ariel. "Michael," he said, "we need to land somewhere. Ariel will lose his wing." If an angel loses a wing, they become part mortal and the other half, well, better to be a dead angel than that.

They had to fly as fast as they could but Lucifer was in hot pursuit. Michael passed Thutmose to Jophiel and turned heel to fly back towards Lucifer. The angels sped on and turned east to find somewhere to rest and repair Ariel's wing. Usually, angels can repair themselves, but this wasn't a normal situation they had found themselves in, and bites from some of Lucifer's creations could be as poisonous as a black adder.

As they landed, Raphael appeared. "You lot had a narrow escape. God has sent me to deal with Ariel. Where's Michael?"

"He went back for Lucifer," said Raguel. Raphael said nothing. It wouldn't matter what he thought, they would all pick up on it anyway. You didn't have private thoughts as an angel, unless you were Michael.

Michael flew fast and could see Lucifer a short distance away. He closed his mind and landed on the ground. Lucifer swung round and crashed into the ground, making it vibrate. He stood up and began walking fast and meaningfully towards Michael. Michael braced himself; the smack that came with Lucifer's tail sent him reeling. Michael slammed into rocks on the side of the mountain. He picked himself up. He could shield himself but this time, this was real. He could feel the hatred pulsating from Lucifer. "Is that all you've got, Luci? Is that as fast as you could go? Perhaps you need to get your skateboard. Oh, wait a minute. Would the god of all hellfire and fury really own a skateboard?"

SMACK… Michael was lifted up and slammed back down. The earth shook again. "Come on, Luci. You can do better than that, can't you?"

Lucifer was draining. The flight, his anger, rage and fury, the strength he was using to lift Michael was all taking its toll. He stood panting in front of Michael, his rippling red and black skin moving like worms around his body.

"It's too late, Lucifer, we have him back. You'll never get him now."

SMACK... Michael was slammed back against the rocks. They cracked, the rocks crumbled. Then suddenly Michael was surrounded by dwarves and they were hanging onto his wings. He was powerless to move; the weight was like boulders. Lucifer turned into the Devil he was and took large strides towards Michael. He stood over him. "I loved you, Michael," he said, "and when I first came here, I missed you so much. I thought that even as a god, I would probably die of a broken heart. I was hoping you would state my case and bring me home. But I've had a long time, Michael. A long time to think about everything you did, and don't ask for forgiveness, I don't have any forgiveness left. You took everything from me and now I'm going to take everything from you. All that spiritual energy God has given you so liberally, I'm going to drain it from you, Michael. Your energy and my energy will merge and I will be able to fool God into thinking I am you. He will be crushed when he sees his favourite son take his kingdom from him. He will be crushed to think it could happen twice. Close your eyes because knock, knock, Mikey. Luci is coming in."

Michael looked up at Lucifer. "I still love you, Lucifer," he said, "and I really thought you had turned a page when you let us take Thutmose."

Lucifer let a tear fall from his eye and he caught it. It turned into a diamond, at least that was what it looked like. "See this, Mikey? It's glass, just glass," said Lucifer. "It false, just like you."

Lucifer stretched forward and put his hand on Michael's head. He closed his eyes and suddenly there was an almighty crack of lightning and the brightest light shone down, singeing Lucifer's wings. "NO!" bellowed a voice.

Lucifer reeled backwards and turned into his angelic self. The light had cast out his demon. "He belongs to me and you shall not touch him, Lucifer. This is exactly what caused your destruction. You never knew when to stop. Back away or I will burn you up completely and you will cease to exist."

Lucifer stood up. "Then do it, Father, anything is better than this. I want to come home."

There was silence for a second and in a moment, Michael was gone. The light disappeared and Lucifer was utterly alone. His dwarves lay in ashes about his feet. "Shadows and dust, Lucifer," God whispered. "That is your kingdom."

Lucifer dropped to his knees and swore revenge, then he got up and went and had a whiskey or two.

CHAPTER 4

"How is your wing, Ariel?" God asked.

"Oh it's fine, Father," he said. "Raphael did a good job."

Raphael smiled. "Anything to help."

God gathered all 12 of the angels around. Thutmose was asleep, levitated in the air.

"Now," God looked at the angels, "does anyone want to tell me about energy?"

Metatron stepped forward, standing proud with his hands behind his back, looking like a major in the army. "Well, in physics, energy is the quantitative property that must be transferred to an object in order to perform work on it or to heat the object." He beamed at being so clever.

God smiled. "Quite right, my son, but in this case, completely wrong."

"I'm never wrong," said Metatron haughtily.

"Er, what now?" said God.

"Sorry, Father. I meant, I'm never wrong about physics."

God laughed. "Does anyone else want to try? Something has happened here, and not one of you, including you, Michael, or you, Metatron, have registered what the issue is. Now, think."

They all huddled together and nominated a spokesman. "We think it has something to do with the sun," said Raphael.

"Well, you would be wrong," said God. "Try again, think

47

more in the vein of something I have given you and what you should think about doing with it."

They huddled together again and Raguel stepped forward. "Father, I think I have the answer. You gave us all a skill…"

"Yes," said God.

"And it was something that you thought we would excel at…"

"Yes…" said God…

"Is it rugby?"

"Oh, for Heaven's sake, no, Raguel, it is not," he answered in a slightly raised voice. "All of you, sit down." They levitated in a seated position. "Right, I'll give you a clue. It means you will last eternally."

"Eternal life," said Michael.

"Yes," said God. "Now, there is something special about Thutmose. What is it?"

"He is the son of Lucifer," said Michael.

"Yes," said God. Ariel pushed Michael's arm and give him the thumbs up. "Michael, perhaps you should not answer any more questions," suggested God.

"Ha, ha," smirked Zadkiel.

God ignored him. "Now, what happens when an immoveable object meets an irresistible force?" Blank faces stared back at God. "Well, it creates an unimaginable event, doesn't it?" Blank faces continued to stare back at God. He loved his children, but they clearly hadn't caught up on his teachings over the millennia. He sighed. "OK, let's try a different approach. If you put half of something onto half of something else, say one half of chocolate onto another half of chocolate, what do you get?"

"Sick," said Raziel. "I had a whole bar of chocolate last

night; I was puking up in the desert all morning."

"You shouldn't really eat chocolate," said Jeremiel. "It isn't good for angels. Strange, that, isn't it? We are angels and we can't eat chocolate? Why is that, Father?"

"Because… Oh for goodness' sake, forget the chocolate. Let's say it was an apple, for instance. If you have half an apple and then put another half with it, what do you get?"

"Trouble in the Garden of Eden," said Uriel. "That's what started all the human stuff in the first place."

"STOP," said God. "It's obvious none of you have taken a blind bit of notice of anything over the millennia. How mankind gets by on your help baffles me, it absolutely baffles me! I'll tell you what you have done." God's size began to increase so he stopped shouting and began to breathe in and out and eventually, he was back to angel size. "Right, this is what has happened, now be quiet until I finish."

The angels were very quiet.

"I appreciate that you wanted to give me a gift for my birthday. The energy you put into the Lapis Lazuli was taken from all of you. You are all immortal and so, you will never die. Do you follow me so far?" The angels nodded. "Now pay attention." They all leaned forward at the same time with their chins on their hands. God looked away before he laughed. "Thutmose is the son of not just Lucifer." They all took a deep breath in.

"Father, who else did the deed?" said Loki. "I will smite him down—"

"Just let me finish, please?" They all sat back up at the same time. "We don't need any smiting just yet, Loki. Now, Thutmose is not just the son of Lucifer, he is in fact the son of a god."

"Which god?" said Gabriel.

"I give up," said God. "Forget I said anything."

"Father, let me explain," said Michael. "I think I know where this is going."

Michael stood up and faced the angels. "Lucifer is an angel and a god. He is the father of Thutmose. Thutmose was therefore born of a god. He is half Lucifer and is, actually was, half human. When we created the Lapis Lazuli stone of life, we put our own immortal energy into it. When it transferred, it completed the other half of Thutmose. That is why he did not die. He couldn't. We have just made a god. He doesn't really need the thousand years because now he is immortal, he will live forever."

There was a groan from all the angels. God placed his hand on Michael's shoulder. "Well done, my son. So you see," said God, "I cannot intervene. Creating a god is not the same as creating a human. A human is born and dies in the passage of time; Thutmose must remain as he is. He will carry on as an immortal, but it is up to you now. You must guide him and bring him to the reality of his situation. I will now change time. We will put Thutmose back exactly where he was before he found the Lapis Lazuli, except the energy has now been expended, and it will no longer be there for him to find; he is already all that it was. He will waken as if from a dream and will carry on his life as though nothing has happened. In 20 years, when people notice there has been no change in him, you will take it in turns to visit him as if human, and try to guide him through. He must not be told that he is immortal, it could push him over the edge. He must reach that milestone in his own time."

Lucifer sat in his kingdom and lay back in his chair. All he had to do now was wait. He had told Thutmose that he would see him again when he was a child, but it would be more fun to see him as he got older. As Lucifer was created by God, sometimes he could listen in on what was happening, indeed that's how he managed to create havoc in the world. He smiled and tapped his fingers on his chair.

God passed Thutmose to Michael. "Take him back, Michael. I will move time. Things will be exactly as they were before. Place him where he fell and he will think he drank too much. He will probably have a banging headache, but it will subside. I have another job to do, now, on your way." Michael picked Thutmose up and God clapped his hands. "Right, everyone, as you were."

Ariel rolled his eyes, "Why does he…"

"Because I can, Ariel," God said. "Because I can." He smiled and pulled his gun finger out with a click of his mouth and a wink of his eye.

In a nanosecond, God was in Hell. Lucifer jumped up from his seat. "What are you doing here? This is my kingdom!"

"Have you really learned nothing, Lucifer?" God asked. "Is this where you intend to spend eternity through your own arrogance and stupidity?" He didn't let Lucifer answer. "I am going to warn you, Lucifer, and you will listen to what I have to say. Thutmose is back on Earth and yes, I know you were listening. You are still my son but I am warning you. Do not, under any circumstances, remove Thutmose from Earth. If you do, you will feel the wrath of my anger. If you go anywhere near him, you will feel the wrath of my anger. I will destroy you utterly, Lucifer. I have tolerated your time on Earth because my love and compassion for you knows no boundaries. I do not want to restrict your activities because your actions help mankind to find their paths. But as Thutmose is your son, he is also mine. Should you try to take him, I will ensure that you spend the rest of your days as a toad possessed with weeping warts and flies, maggots will crawl over you for eternity. Your kingdom will be no more. Do I make myself clear? I will bring you to an end sooner than your time."

Lucifer stood up and faced God. He had no idea what Lucifer had planned. How could he? The plan had been perfected and was hidden inside his mind, which he had become a master at hiding. He transformed into the angel that God had created. "Yes, Father, crystal, but is it not a selfish thing to do? I have no family now; you are taking my son from me. I can have no contact with him? Who would do that to a parent?"

"Do not try me, Lucifer," said God. "I have made my ruling, but I will adjust this by one point. You may view him from a distance and that is all. You may watch him and IF you can intervene to improve his lot in life, without being totally ridiculous, then I will accept that, but remember what I said, Lucifer. This is non-negotiable."

"But Father…" It was too late, God had gone. Lucifer sat down. "Touché," he said, and slid back into his demon form.

CHAPTER 5

Michael laid Thutmose down and stepped away. He felt affection for Thutmose; he would never know that he had angels fighting for him and it would be years before he knew what was in store for him. Michael heard God. "Coming, Father," and he was gone.

As the sun rose over the large pyramid, Thutmose had the biggest headache he had ever encountered; he felt like his head would explode and why did he smell of sulphur? He sniffed his clothes. With a headache like this he must have been in a bar all night and embarrassingly, he had passed out not far from his crew. As he stood up, he wavered and suddenly vomited. He had a sense of déjà vu but wasn't sure why.

"Morning, boss." Some of his crew were laughing and waving in his direction. "Good night last night?"

Thutmose put up his hand. "You really shouldn't have let me drink so much," he said.

"Well we wouldn't have, but you weren't with us last night. A big old elderly bloke dropped you where you were. We thought you might have been too drunk to tell him where you lived."

Must have been a good night, Thutmose thought. *I really do not remember that bit at all. What big old man? Oh well, I'll just make sure I don't get that drunk again.* Thutmose had no idea that he would never be drunk again, because he was a god and gods don't imbibe alcohol and end up getting drunk. There were lots of other things they didn't do either, but he had life after life to learn about it.

By lunchtime he was feeling much better and was becoming increasingly pleased with the pyramid. It was being built for Khufu, the second king of the 4th dynasty. It was the largest of what would be three. The length of each side at the base would average 755.75 feet (230 metres) and its height would be 481.4 feet (147 metres). There would be secrets held within this pyramid that only he and one or two others would know. He felt very important.

He noticed whilst looking at the dimensions of a drawing on some papyrus paper that there was a man staring at him. He looked up and the man was a very grand Egyptian. He was very large and Thutmose tried to look away but he kept looking back. *I wonder if it's the same man from last night,* he thought. Geb smiled and motioned for him to come to him. Thutmose looked around but everyone was working. He looked back and the man motioned him to come to him again. Thutmose put the papyrus down and made his way over. "Can I help you?" he said.

"Not really, no," said Geb, "but I can help you. Walk with me. I have something to show you."

"I'm working," said Thutmose.

"Yes you are," Geb smiled and slapped his back, "but truth be known, you really don't need to." Thutmose was very confused and felt that he knew this person, that there had been some sort of interaction with him before but he didn't know what. "Please," said Geb and held his arm ahead to point the way.

"Is there never any peace?" said Michael.

Metatron smiled. "Leave this to me, Michael. I'll deal with this," and off he shot.

"He's very bloody fast," said Ariel.

"Practice," said Michael, and walked away smiling. Of course, it wasn't practice, God had given him the gift of speed.

"I could really hate you, Michael!" shouted Ariel to his back.

"No you couldn't!" Michael shouted back.

Ariel thought to himself, *He's right, I could never hate him.*

"Course I'm right!" shouted Michael, laughing.

Ariel was less than amused and decided to go and beat a human at a game of tug of war to make himself feel better.

Geb walked next to Thutmose, smiling and making small comments about the work on the pyramid. Thutmose smiled. "Look, is there something you want to say? I really am so very busy. This large pyramid is for Khufu, you know, the Pharaoh of Egypt. He pays all our wages. I don't want to be rude… I feel like I know you, but I don't, if you know what I mean? But I need to…"

Geb grinned. "I know exactly what you mean, you see, you think you just woke up here this morning and everything was how you expected it to be, didn't you?"

Thutmose, slightly bemused, was just about to answer when a voice boomed, "And you would be absolutely right. Zeb, my old friend, how are you? I haven't seen you in a long time. Let's go and drink and talk about old days." Metatron had turned into an Egyptian gentleman and was also dressed in finery.

Geb rolled his eyes. "Old days?" He shook his head, irritated. "No, don't know who you are or what you mean." Geb pulled Thutmose by the arm, trying to bypass people and walk into the desert.

"You know, old days, like being old like we are, the two of us, older men, talking about the past and things we did, battles, women, men drinking, muscles, GRRRRRRRR." Metatron flexed his muscles and was trying to keep up with Geb but having to walk sideways like a crab, through the people.

"No, don't know you," established Geb, wheeling his finger next to his temple and telling Thutmose Metatron was a mad man.

"What about the wife, does she know you're here? You are still married to, who was it now, ah yes, Nut?"

Thutmose stopped and looked at Geb. "Nut? What like the goddess Nut?"

"NOOOOOO," said Geb. "Her name is Nutalina, very nice girl from Jordan. Nut or Nutty for short."

Metatron suppressed a giggle. "You're telling me." He grinned.

Geb looked at Metatron. "Move along now, my man, we're trying to talk about important things here."

"Well, I think this is one conversation I should be involved in. I probably know more about 'things' than most people, for instance, do you know how much time someone can be locked inside a frozen block of ice for? Let's say their temperature drops to 0 or even less?"

Thutmose chipped in, "They would have to be superhuman for that."

"You have no idea," said Metatron and looked back at Geb. Metatron had stopped smiling.

"But supposing someone has a friend who has a ball of fire or a very large candle that could melt it?" Geb challenged Metatron.

"Then," he smiled, "I suggest we go and find him, because I'm guessing he isn't too far from here, and we can ask him what he thinks. But I would also guess that he knows an even bigger person who has probably told him to not intervene." Metatron was raising his voice. "So what are your thoughts on that?" Metatron folded his arms.

"Well supposing… just supposing it was someone with a chariot that could race across a sunny sky and melt everything and everyone?" Metatron frowned quizzically at Geb who stopped and realised he had just lost this argument. He knew better than to tangle words with Metatron, and gallantly excused himself from the company of Thutmose. "It looks like my friend here wants to talk about mathematics and science. I will see you again, young man." He slapped Thutmose on the shoulder. Both Geb and Metatron walked away into the crowd.

WOW, thought Thutmose, making his way back to the pyramid. *That was really weird.*

Geb looked at Metatron. "Zeb? Who the hell is Zeb?"

Metatron laughed. "Look, we can't afford for Thutmose to find out yet just who he is and what he is doing here. I have a sneaky feeling you could be working for the enemy, and if you continue on that road, you *will* lose. God is all over it at the moment. Really, how's Nut?"

Geb looked at Metatron. "You really don't need me to answer that question, do you?" Geb looked around him. "Must go. Things to do, my friend, and by the way, Mezzers, did you know Lucifer has a skateboard?"

Metatron tutted. "Your allegiances really are all over the place, Geb. I thought it was Nut who was supposed to be hormonal, not you."

CHAPTER 6

Snefru was, by all accounts, the greatest of all Egyptian pyramid builders and Thutmose was very proud to be working with him. Not only did he feel respected but he felt that he could perhaps take Snefru's place one day, if the gods were willing. He hoped that one day he would be as good as, or even better than, his mentor. Snefru used to tell Thutmose that he was indeed blessed by the gods.

There had been an incident two years earlier when a large rock, being pulled by the teams up the path on the pyramid, had flipped sideways and fell to the ground, narrowly missing Thutmose. Thutmose had sensed it at the last second and dived out of the way of it at lighting speed. It was so fast that people thought the gods themselves must have moved him. Thutmose felt slightly sick after the movement. Snefru told him it was the gods; they wanted him alive to help finish the pyramids. Thutmose had no idea where the abilities came from but in time, he would learn to control the speed so it wouldn't leave him with motion sickness.

One evening, Thutmose was sitting watching the sun go down, then Snefru came to sit with him. "Beautiful sunset tonight." Snefru pointed with his hand.

Thutmose laughed. "It's a beautiful sunset every night. Not sure why I watch it, to be honest." Snefru handed him some wine; Thutmose moved it away. "Sorry, I'm not feeling particularly sociable tonight. I can't drink," he said. "I get really bad memory loss. I could kill someone and not know about it."

Snefru shrugged. "So what? Life is too short, Thutmose; the gods are laughing at us because they know our time is short. Drink to your life and sod the gods." He passed the wine back to Thutmose.

Thutmose drank but didn't really enjoy the taste. He drank again and still didn't particularly enjoy it, but it was better than sitting alone. He passed it back to Snefru. "I'm not enjoying it," he said.

"Well, maybe you are already drunk," laughed Snefru, and decided to stay with his friend and try to cheer him up. Through the night they talked, joked, laughed and drank wine. Snefru became more and more indiscreet about the pyramids and what was expected when they were finished, and Thutmose became more and more aware that it didn't matter how much he drank, he wasn't getting drunk. He supposed it was the quality of the wine and perhaps he would feel it in the morning.

Snefru told Thutmose about his wife, his sons, his home. His wife was pregnant again and it was supposed she would have a female child. Was Thutmose planning on a family? Thutmose had not really given much thought to the future. He had dated the odd female here and there but it had never turned into anything because he had not given it the time it needed and to be honest, he did not really want a relationship. He felt that there was more to be had in life and anyway, men lived to old ages, and many had young wives, so he might marry later in life and think about that type of thing then. He wanted to see more of the world and be involved in some way, maybe to make a difference to it.

As they talked, Thutmose became aware of a voice. It was an unhappy voice, then it was a happy voice, then it spoke of secrets, but the voice was sporadic and it sounded like it was next to him. He could not really make out what it was saying, yet Snefru was next to him, so what was it? Thutmose sat up, straining to hear, but it went quiet.

"What is it?" said Snefru. "Can you hear something?"

Thutmose looked around. "I think I can hear something, but I'm not sure what… I think it must be the wine."

Snefru grunted and drank back some more wine. "Well, I think I will be going home to my wife who will not be happy about the late hour I am keeping. It is a good job I have a hard head and money to buy more pots. We will need them when I get home, I think." Snefru laughed and having slapped Thutmose on the shoulder, he staggered towards the miniature city close to the large pyramid. Snefru felt a pang of guilt in his stomach. Thutmose had no idea what was in store for him and he had left him before the wine made him let the secret out. Thutmose would have a long life, he presumed, but not on this earth.

Thutmose waved back at Snefru, but sat perfectly still. The voice had disappeared but he was certain that he heard it. Maybe he was going mad. He stayed a little longer and watched as the night sky changed its hue and more stars appeared, like someone had an implement and was poking holes in a dark blanket and letting the light through. Thutmose stared at the night sky; he could make out different constellations and fancied he could name them all if he wanted to, but he had not played that game for a long time. He couldn't recall ever having been taught what they were, though he remembered some elderly man in the past who seemed to be able to teach him things, but he had not seen him for many years. Tall man, very strong, but somehow seemed very young and yet ancient too.

In the darkness Lucifer watched. He was aching to speak to his son, but he felt a power much stronger than he was and he knew who it was and where it was coming from. He slithered back into the darkness to melt in with the shadows. He watched Thutmose and wanted to tell him what was happening to him, but knew the consequences of such an approach.

Thutmose dusted himself down and decided he needed a walk; he would walk to Cairo. Cairo was always awake when humans slept, and awake when humans were awake. He smiled at his own thought. Cairo never seemed to sleep. As he began to walk he felt like he needed to exhaust himself and so he began to run. He felt a sense of relief; he wanted the stress and strains of the day to dissolve. As he ran, he sensed the muscles and sinews in his body, he felt the blood coursing through his veins, his muscles were appreciating the exercise he was giving them, he felt he could run faster and so he did. He suddenly became aware that he was running quite fast and made himself stop. It was curious to him that he wasn't perspiring and he wasn't tired, he wasn't even puffing for more air. He had literally just decided to stop and it was as if he had been standing or sitting still for hours. He wasn't the slightest bit tired. Thutmose looked around and was stunned to see how far he had run. Uncomfortable now, he wondered if anyone had noticed him. He could see nothing, so he began a slow jog, he then picked up his pace and before he knew it, he was running extremely fast again. He was on the outskirts of Cairo and it had taken him hardly any time to arrive there. He stopped again and looked around; he knew this wasn't normal. He felt excited, but scared at the same time. Was it his diet? Was it the heavy lifting work? Was he just getting more fit with each passing day? He did not know, but he felt like he could keep running and nothing would tire him out.

From the edge of the desert, Bastet had noticed him. She was interested to see how far he had come in the years, but being a son of Lucifer, she didn't want to get too involved. She just wanted to have a look at this fine figure. She decided to follow him to see where he was going on this cool balmy evening. He was very handsome and she smiled coyly to herself. Changing quickly into a cat, she flicked her tail and ran towards him. "Well, hello, pretty kitty." But he thought it rather unusual for a cat to be on the edge of the desert and running alongside him, and being able to keep up? Perhaps it was a lucky cat? Perhaps his luck would change? It was a beautiful black cat with penetrating emerald-green eyes.

He jogged to the edge of the city of Cairo. He bent down to stroke the cat, and Bastet rubbed herself all over his legs. Unable to resist, he picked her up and she bumped her head into his face and began to purr. "You are very friendly." He smiled and rubbed his head to her head. He put her carefully back down, stroking the long lovely fur length of her body. Bastet arched her back approvingly. "On your way home then, little lovely," he said, and then walked slowly through the bustling marketplace.

Bastet turned and looked at him and slowly blinked her eyes. She flicked her tail. "I'll definitely be seeing him again," she purred. She turned a corner where no one could see her and disappeared.

The market never slept and neither did most of the Egyptians, it seemed. They all slept at different times. Thutmose loved the market. So many goods were being sold; lots of different mysteries came in from the ships and made their way to the markets. He just loved being in amongst the people and observing what they did and what they bought. The bartering that went on at the stalls was a favourite of his, it was like a contest to see who could get away with the most, or least money. He watched the stall holders as they put their hands to their faces when asked for a cheaper price. Their moans of horror, their poor families, grandmothers, children who would have to go without if they reduced their prices. The dramas that unfolded were a thing to behold. He carried on walking through the market lost in a haze of brass, gold, light, stone, chattering. Fine clothes that looked fit for kings. Coming towards him was a woman dressed in the very best finery, and with her were three women who were keeping her cool in the warm night air, waving palm leaves above her. They were showing her things she pointed at on the stalls. As Thutmose passed, the woman looked at him and smiled when she walked by. He nodded but kept walking. He wasn't in the mood for idle conversation and he knew it wouldn't come to anything. She was married, but how did he know that?

"You keep watch, I will knock her to the ground and steal her basket. People will never catch us. Pretend to chase me and we will meet at the beginning of the desert." Thutmose stopped. Where did that come from? He had heard a voice as though it was next to him. Perhaps it was someone next to him. He looked around but nothing seemed out of place.

People were going about their business. He walked on. "I will go now, go and linger by the lamp stall. I will knock her over, you must chase me to make it look like you are trying to help. The old lady is wearing red, she is stumbling and looks alone, she looks like easy prey."

Thutmose stopped. Was this a joke? He looked around and he saw an elderly lady wearing red who was struggling to walk. He watched her, then he noticed a man lingering by a light stall who was watching her uneasily. A feeling in the pit of his stomach told him he was looking at the man who was about to assault and rob the old woman. Confidently, Thutmose walked up to him and said, "If you touch that old lady, I will break your arms and legs so badly, you will not be able to beg for your food. You will starve to death and your body will be buried in a bin."

The man looked shocked and moved away, nearly stumbling himself as he walked backwards away from Thutmose. Thutmose stared after him and felt an anger he had never felt before, one that was truly harsh and brutal and he fancied if he let it get out of control, there would be no stopping it. Thutmose's arms began to feel like they were shaking. Lucifer was watching from a distance and put his hand to his mouth to stifle the giggle. "Like father, like son," he snickered.

Thutmose noticed the intended robber was joined by another older man, and they were looking uneasily in his direction. They looked puzzled but moved out of sight. Thutmose caught sight of the old lady again and followed her at a discreet distance. He knew she was going home and he walked in the shadows until she reached the door of her house so as not to alarm her. She opened her door and dragged her tired old body inside. He heard a click; he assumed it was the lock. Smiling, he started out towards the desert.

"There he is, follow him." The voices were disembodied but he knew the men were close by. He hid in the shadows and waited for them. "Where is he?" said the man he had seen by the lighting stand.

Thutmose moved quickly. "I'm right behind you."

As they both turned around, he grabbed them and banged their heads together. He felt the shockwave through his hands and both men fell to the ground. Though no one saw it, and Thutmose never knew it, his eyes had flashed red. Lucifer was in the darkness and chuckled with delight. Thutmose pondered on what had just happened. He would never have approached those two men on his own under normal circumstances. This had been a very strange evening. What was happening to him? Hearing voices? Running at speed with a cat, taking on two robbers. He really did think he was losing his mind. There was an elderly woman who lived on the outskirts of the pyramid village; she seemed to know much about many things. He decided that tomorrow, he would pay her a visit. He ran back to Pyramid City and joined his friends. He decided that he was going to get extremely drunk.

CHAPTER 7

The sun was high and the day was hot. Thutmose had arisen without a headache and felt happier than he had the day before. He felt the walk to Cairo and his good deed had made the world seem a better place. He thought perhaps that the voices he had heard and his running quickly were figments of his imagination after a long and stressful day. He smiled; he had taken things far too seriously and should just accept his lot in life and not worry about silly concerns. He joined Snefru and they continued to discuss the work for the day. They looked over the plans and decided who would head the teams for hauling the slabs up the runways. They were one man short due to sickness so Thutmose said he would head a team.

He walked up the runway and he ordered the team to pull. Below them were a group of workers who were organising their slabs and carts. Suddenly, and without warning, a section of the rope snapped and at great speed the slab was sliding down the side of the pyramid. Thutmose saw it was heading towards workmen. "Slaaaaaaaab!" he yelled. They looked up and ran. The slab shattered into pieces and became nothing more than crumbling stones running down the side of the pyramid. The team turned and looked at Thutmose. It was his shouting that had shattered the stone, they were certain of it. His voice had been unusually loud and they had seen the slab vibrate. They looked genuinely afraid and began to move away from him. "What?" he said.

Snefru quickly took control of the situation. He had seen what was happening. He ran towards the pyramid; they could not afford to stop work. "Faulty slab!" shouted Snefru. "It will need recutting. I told them to make sure that each slab was perfect."

People looked round, confused, glancing between each other. None of the slabs had ever shattered that badly, if at all. "What?" said Thutmose.

"I said faulty slab." Snefru put his hands on his hips. "It's happened before. Certain parts of the quarry produce slabs that once they decide to slide and shatter, well there's nothing you can do about it. Back down, men, please, we need to choose a better one. Khufru won't be happy if we use faulty stone." He glanced at Thutmose who was still stunned and wasn't sure what had happened. "I think you need a drink," said Snefru. "We nearly lost a few men. In fact, I think the whole team need a drink. Ropes down, let's go."

The team seemed to be coming around but as they walked down the pyramid they glanced at the stone, they glanced at Thutmose and whispers began circulating amongst them. "I said move, now, please," said Snefru.

The team came down and sat on the sand. Each man was handed a drink. They glanced uneasily at Thutmose who was taken to one side by Snefru. "Thutmose, take the afternoon off. The loss of the stone has spooked the men and two workers have left. They have mentioned stories of spells and witchcraft. Stupidity, I know and you know, but come back tomorrow, we will start the day anew. It WAS a faulty stone." Snefru slapped Thutmose thoughtlessly on his back; he needed to get the teams moving again. He didn't think for a minute that it was a faulty stone. He wasn't sure what had happened but he needed to get the job done, he needed his salary.

Thutmose wasn't happy, but he was going to do what Snefru said. He picked up his ruckbag and walked towards the desert to see the old lady. Snefru watched Thutmose as he left. The sooner the job was done and all the spare ends finished, the better. He shouted for the team to start moving again.

Thutmose walked towards the house of the old lady. As he approached an icy draft went before him. It was thirty-seven degrees, but he wasn't going to question an icy draft. He had felt too much in the last two days to question anything now. He stood outside the cloth door of the old lady's house. He was wondering what he was doing there and suddenly felt very stupid. He turned to walk away when a voice shouted, "Come in, Thutmose, have a tea with me." He turned. Did he hear that? Did the voice really shout or was it in his head? How did she know his name? He decided to leave, then the voice shouted again, "Come in, Thutmose, have a tea with me." He turned around and walked towards the cloth door. He moved it to one side. The old lady had her hair in a plait and her dress was a long, grey, sack cloth. She had sandals on her feet and scarcely anything in her house. She smiled and seemed very grandmother like. Thutmose felt at ease. She motioned for him to sit down. "So, bad today then?" she ventured. Thutmose looked quizzically at her. She waved her hand at him. "Uh, I can hear and see more here than you think. It's a very interesting place to live – the noise carries." Thutmose wasn't going to question the distance, even if he was mathematically gifted. She passed the tea to him and he put it down on the stone table in her living room. She sat back and looked at him. "I know exactly why you are here," she told him. Thutmose still didn't say anything, he was still in shock from the events of the day. "I will let you drink your tea, then we will talk." He gave a half nod in agreement and picked up his cup.

The black tea was hot and the steam filled his eyes. He felt an overwhelming sense of emotion. His mind went back to his first memory of coming into the world. He recalled a light, a very bright light; there was pain on his cheek where he had been bitten by a snake and he remembered crying but suddenly falling asleep. How could he remember these things? He was a baby, a child. He couldn't remember his mother – she had died in childbirth. He had struggled growing up with only his father as support. He felt no love from the old man, but had felt the back of his hand a few times. Thutmose had grown up a hardened child and won every fight he ever had with other children. This was how he had gained respect from the other children. As he got older, the fights got harder but he never lost and he never seemed to bruise for long and cuts healed easily. When he reached his late teens, he had decided that he needed a trade and had taken time to serve under a stone cutter who cut hieroglyphs for the Pharaoh's tombs, and this is where he met Snefru, who had taken him under his wing.

He sobbed heavily and felt lost. He didn't know who he was anymore. The sobbing shook his body, but the old lady didn't comfort him, she just continued to drink her tea and take in every emotion that he emitted. She knew exactly who he was; she had been born millennia ago herself and this old lady he saw, was covered by an illusory body which hid who she really was. Iside stood up and went into the kitchen.

Thutmose would cease sobbing in a few moments. Although she wanted to comfort him, she would not touch the son of the Devil. He could extract energy from her in seconds and she would age and die. She had come close to that eventuality many eons ago when Lucifer fooled her into thinking he would be her partner for eternity. He had shielded himself from her. It was her energy he wanted; it was only with the intervention of Bastet that it had stopped, but it had left Iside in a deep sleep for two hundred years. She owed Bastet her life. She knew that Thutmose wouldn't do it on purpose, but he was his father's son and they shared memories, he might get greedy. No, she would need to keep under wraps who she was and tread carefully.

She returned to her living space and Thutmose was now silent again. "I am sorry," he said. "If you want me to leave…?" Iside smiled. She knew how difficult it was to come to terms with being a god, especially when it was not your fault. She had met this type of new god before.

"Have you finished your tea?" she said. Thutmose nodded. "Good," she said, "now close your eyes and put your head back and listen to my voice." Thutmose did as she asked. Why, he did not know, but it was the tea, it made people more acquiescent. "Who are you?" said Iside.

Thutmose put his head up and looked at her. "You know who I am?" he quizzed.

Iside looked at him; her bright blue eyes seem to sparkle. "Put your head back, Thutmose." He leaned back again and felt more comfortable. "Search your soul, and find yourself," prompted Iside.

Thutmose wasn't sure what she meant, but he calmed himself down, relaxed and began to ask questions of his soul.

He asked who he was, where he came from, what his purpose in life was, where should he be, where should he live, but sometimes a black cloud pervaded his mind. He struggled to get through it. Faces he did not know flashed in and out of his mind. They seemed to be faces of gods and angels. *Impossible*, he told his mind. He had a very deep spiritual feeling that filled him with joy, happiness and laughter, but then he felt rage, anger, despair, and more baser instincts that he tried to control. His hands curled up into fists. He was in a deep state of meditation and he felt like he was experiencing out-of-body movements. He was back at the pyramids watching what was happening; he stood over Snefru whilst he looked at plans. Snefru was puzzled and he heard him thinking about Thutmose and needing his counsel. He walked through the men around the pyramid, who now seemed to think they had seen something and nothing and they still considered Thutmose their friend. They hoped he was well and would be back the next day.

Thutmose wandered around in a spiritual haze and then saw a darkness he could not penetrate. He wasn't afraid of it, indeed there was something in there he wanted to see but he just could not get through. Lucifer felt what was happening and withdrew further into the darkness. "Bugger," he said.

The angels in Heaven felt what was happening. Thutmose was searching. They gathered together and stood and watched. God broke into their thoughts. "Metatron and Michael, it has nearly been twenty Earth years. You need to visit Thutmose and break to him gently who he is. When that is done, you will all take responsibility for showing him the right path. Remember this will be a shock for him and it needs to be done with great compassion, consideration and thoughtfulness."

Lucifer was listening and he wanted to be involved. God had given him permission to help if it would help Thutmose's purpose. Lucifer needed to think on this very carefully.

Iside called Thutmose back; the quiet liquid softness of her voice was calling his name. His soul turned and saw a beautiful goddess – she was incredible. He moved purposefully towards her. He wanted to touch her, to see if she was real. The colours moved in and out of her like a liquid rainbow; they merged and sparkled, then suddenly jolted, he was awake, back in the same room with the elderly woman. "How are you feeling?" Iside asked him.

Thutmose looked puzzled. "I'm a bit confused about what I have seen, but I feel much calmer now. I feel like I know more about myself but there were things I didn't understand. Are you…?" He was about to say 'a goddess' but Iside stopped him so she wouldn't be encouraged to answer.

"I am an old woman who helps people come to terms with upsetting issues in their lives," she said. "Now I will give you a riddle and when you have solved it, you will know who you are."

Thutmose frowned. "I am Thutmose, I work at the pyramids," he said.

Iside smiled. She laid her hand on his hand and Thutmose passed out. Iside shone, her eyes glistened. It was such a relief to get out of the mortal body; it was like being strapped inside a mummy case. She sat opposite Thutmose and her radiance filled the room. "Thutmose," she whispered.

Friends and family will die, I will not cry.

I am a son, I am a god, my heritage I have forgot.

I will know how to lie, I am immortal, I will not die.

I am born, I am old, I am searching, searching, searching…

Thutmose woke up on the edge of the desert. "Damn," he said. "I really have to stop getting drunk." He sat up, dusted himself off and decided to walk into Cairo. He changed his mind and ran.

CHAPTER 8

It was the final few days before the pyramid would be finished. Pharaoh had decided that there would be a big party on the day that it finished and it would likely go on long into the night. Everyone would be able to have their fill of food and drink, on the orders of the Pharaoh. The incident at the pyramid had been long forgotten and everyone accepted Thutmose back into the pyramid family. Snefru had noticed many things about Thutmose, but the biggest was that in the twenty years of building the pyramid, he had not changed. There were no extra wrinkles, no grey hairs, yet time here always took its toll. There were men far younger than Thutmose who looked older than him. Thutmose should at least be approaching 40 and he looked no older than 25. Snefru was, without doubt, jealous. There was something Thutmose had that kept him young. Snefru wasn't sure what it was, but he wanted it. He approached Thutmose with these thoughts in mind and invited him out for the evening in Cairo. Thutmose accepted Snefru's offer and as they walked Snefru asked questions about his family life. Thutmose was slightly confused because Snefru had known him for years and knew almost all there was to know about his family.

He kept walking with Snefru and a voice said, "Be careful. All is not as it seems." Rather than baulk at the sound of the voice, Thutmose listened. Snefru seemed different tonight.

Thutmose wasn't sure how, but his demeanour had changed. "He is jealous of you," the voice said. "Tonight, he is dangerous. You need to go home." Thutmose slowed his walk. Snefru looked confused.

"Something wrong, my friend?"

Thutmose looked at Snefru. "I think perhaps I need to go home," said Thutmose. "I'm suddenly not feeling too sociable. I'm tired. I would not be good company."

Snefru was annoyed but tried not to show it. "We have walked a long way," he said. "We may as well go the rest of the way now."

"Snefru, my friend, please excuse me, I need to go home."

Snefru showed slight irritation but said, "Fine, go. I'll see you tomorrow at the party." Thutmose turned and left. Snefru continued into Cairo where he met up with the men that Thutmose had knocked out weeks before. "He went home," said Snefru. "We will need to go into his home."

The men looked at each other. "Snefru, this man is dangerous. If we got trapped in his house… His eyes flashed red… He is an evil spirit."

"Don't be stupid," said Snefru, "it was the light or the blood buzzing in your heads when he caught you unawares. This man has secrets. He has not aged, I tell you. He should be like us now, but no, he has stayed young. The secret must be hidden in his house and it must be ours. We could be gods and live forever, we could sell the secret and be rich forever. Money, women, houses, donkeys, horses, food, drink…" Snefru was holding their arms and bending in, whispering in excitement. They had drunk alcohol and were feeling brave and invincible. They finished their cups and made their way out towards the desert.

Thutmose closed the door of his house. "It's not over – be careful," said the voice.

Thutmose sat down and closed his eyes. "Who is that?" he said. But no response came. "Tell me who you are. I demand it," Thutmose said, with as much authority as he could muster talking to a disembodied voice. Still no response. He sat quietly but still there was no reply. He did not need to sleep, but decided to. He allowed the waves of tiredness to fill his head and his eyes; he lay back on his couch and fell into a deep sleep. He dreamt of Cairo when he was a young child and his quieter moments when he sat on the edge of the desert looking into nothingness. He dreamt of his work and building the pyramid. He saw two large men walking towards him and in his dream, they looked like angels. They got closer and just as they were about to reach him, he was pulled out his sleep and found himself on his back on the floor, with a knife at his throat.

The man who was holding him was large and had a scarf around his face and head. "Where is it?" he threatened, digging the knife deeper into Thutmose's neck. Snefru, hidden in a scarf, pulled the man's hand away.

Only Snefru's eyes were showing but Thutmose knew immediately who it was. This jolted him up and he began to fight. "Snefru, why are you doing this?" Thutmose was being pushed and pulled; they were trying to pull his hands behind his back. Snefru lost the scarf from around his head during the struggle and so it was now beyond doubt who was accosting him in his own home.

The men shoved Thutmose onto the floor. They were all yelling, "Give us the secret of your immortality." They were shouting, "Give it to us or die!" They had no idea of the contradiction they had just implied.

Thutmose shouted that he didn't know what they were talking about, and as he pushed the fat man away, with a sweep of the knife, the thinner man plunged it into Thutmose's stomach. Everything seemed to move in slow motion. Snefru's eyes widened as he watched Thutmose fall to the floor. The thin man could not believe what he had done; he had never harmed anyone in his life other than to rob them, and he made off out of the door and ran back towards Cairo, stumbling as he ran. He had never been involved in a murder. In the darkness a much more dangerous foe emerged. Lucifer thundered towards the man as he stumbled through the sand and with one swipe of his mighty tail smashed him onto the ground, the body turning to bloody pulp, the mouth moving on its own as the nerves jittered through it. The eyes were flicking and the brain still conscious, realising what had happened, trying to make the mouth scream. Lucifer felt nothing but rage; he had broken a rule again. God was the only one who could take human life, but Lucifer had killed a mortal, his painful scream echoed through the night air. It was too late now. Lucifer would have to finish what he started. He felt God's anger but Lucifer had lost control. He could not go to Thutmose's house because of his promise to God, and as the soul of the crushed corpse rose from the mashed-up mess, Lucifer grabbed it by the throat and swallowed it. It would be regurgitated back in Hell. Lucifer waited for the others to run from Thutmose house, but what he saw stopped him in his tracks. He could not move, he had to stay where he was. Lucifer looked up into the sky. Nothing was returned. No sound, no cry, no voice. He looked back towards what was happening and for the first time in many millennia, he felt powerless to intervene. He could not get close to the men who had harmed his son, without being close to Thutmose.

The two men pulled Thutmose outside of his house. It was in a lone spot so no one saw what was happening. They picked him up and carried him as though he was drunk. It wasn't unusual for Thutmose to have a good night out so they had the opportunity to say he was drunk if anyone asked them. They had partially covered him with a blanket to cover the stain of the blood. They made their way towards to the pyramid and began to dig. The stars were twinkling as they finally felt they had dug far enough. They rolled Thutmose's body into a hole and covered it over. It was safer as all holes and gaps were beginning to be filled in. Thutmose would never be found, at least not in this century. The murderers agreed not to meet for a few days and to go about their business as though nothing had happened. If anyone asked about Thutmose, Snefru would say he had gone on a journey looking for adventure. They would return to Thutmose's house on the pretext of clearing it out, as friends, so others could move in. Thutmose had no family to pass it onto. Maybe Snefru could take it over, as his closest friend. The men parted ways.

As the fat man made his way back towards Cairo, a huge scaly animal, with claws, long teeth and hair, appeared from nowhere. It pinned the large man to the floor on his back and began to eat him slowly, piece by piece. The fat man was so frightened that he wet himself and defecated. Disembowelling him, the poison of the animal's tongue had paralysed him; he could not move, he could only watch his own death. His screams of pain and agony were heard by no one. Lucifer stood in the darkness and watched. When the end had come, the soul tried to run. Lucifer whipped out his tongue and swallowed it. It would meet its friend in Hell, for eternity. He had a very special surprise for Snefru.

In the hole, Thutmose was sleeping. The sand had settled like glass around his body. His body was repairing and he would be awake in hours. Outside the hole sat Metatron and Michael. "You know, Michael?" said Metatron. "You don't want to make a habit of this, waiting for Thutmose to wake up. You're going to get yourself a name."

Michael looked at Metatron who smiled a massive smile. "Whoooooo, angel of death," said Metatron, wiggling his fingers at Michael.

Michael was going to be cross but then laughed, and kept laughing. They both mimicked the 'Whooooo.' Even Loki, the angel of death, laughed. Michael's laugh, the angels have said, should be bottled and sold around the world; it was beautiful and infectious.

In the darkness Lucifer heard Michael's laugh. He began to laugh; memories of Michael and him ran through his mind. He laughed harder and then suddenly, Lucifer began to cry. His tears coursed down his face and, in the darkness, a little spark flickered. He changed from the monster to Lucifer the Angel of Light. Michael and Metatron suddenly stood up.

"Lucifer is around, isn't he?" said Metatron. "I thought I smelled him earlier but I couldn't be sure."

Michael looked directly to where Lucifer was standing. "Yes, he's here but he's not going to fight us, Metatron, and he hasn't come to take Thutmose. Can you keep guard a minute? I will be back." Michael turned and walked directly to where Lucifer was standing. "You can't hide from me, Luci."

Michael smiled.

Lucifer came out of the darkness. He had toned his light down and drew his wings in. "Hello, Mikey," he said.

"Bit of a mess you made." Michael nodded with his head.

"Well it's what I do," he said, "but don't worry, I will clear it up."

"I know," said Michael.

They both stood looking at each other, not quite sure what to say, which was surprising for angels. I've heard it said, you usually can't get them to shut up. Suddenly Michael pulled out a light sword. "En garde, criminal!" he shouted.

Lucifer could have cried with joy. "Have at ye, oh naughty angel. I will have thee on a table and dance on thy grave. En garde!" laughed Lucifer. They put their swords up to their foreheads and they were off. They play fought for over an hour; Lucifer was still trying to cheat. Metatron watched from a distance and smiled. God and the angels watched from above and Geb, Bastet and Iside watched from the desert. To any human, it would have appeared that two fireflies were flying around in circles, up and down, side to side. To immortals, they were two angels, who desperately missed each other's company, forgetting about everything, just for a moment, reverting back to their former childish selves before taking on the task of caring for mankind.

Their joy at their silliness was infectious and was felt deeply by all immortals around the world. Most of them stopped for a moment to take in the happiness they felt being sent out by the angels. Most couldn't believe that Lucifer was capable of sending out such joy, but it was an attribute he could give if he really wanted to, having had it imbued by God when he was created.

Metatron was suddenly brought back to reality as from the corner of his eye, he saw movement in the hole. He looked towards Michael. Michael and Lucifer both picked up the thought form and stopped fighting. Lucifer looked suddenly sad. "Take care of him for me, Michael."

Michael turned and looked at Lucifer. "Hate you, fish face," he said and smiled.

"Hate you more, you ugly bugger," said Lucifer. Michael put his sword up to his head and ran back towards Metatron. "You'll never be as beautiful as me, Michael!" yelled Lucifer. Michael waved his sword.

Lucifer drew back into the darkness. He would go back to Hell now and regurgitate the souls he had collected. The gates of Hell opened for the eyes of immortals only, and Lucifer walked in with his new acquisitions, and he whistled all the way.

CHAPTER 9

Thutmose was moving and Michael and Metatron watched him. The movements were slow and there were a few minutes in between each one.

Michael frowned. "It could be hours yet. He may be stuck in between worlds." They sat down again and waited.

Thutmose could not see properly, then slowly his eyes began to focus. There was a violet glow to his right and he heard a woman's voice.

"Thutmose, walk towards me, follow my voice."

He did not feel afraid and did as the voice asked. As he grew closer, the woman became sharper and the colour fluorescent. He thought he recognised her, then it suddenly dawned on him. "Mother?"

"Hello." She smiled warmly. "I didn't expect to see you so soon, but you do know you can't stay here, don't you?"

Thutmose smiled. "I have a feeling I'm a little different, Mother. Are you going to tell me why?"

"No, I'm not," she said, "but you are finding out what makes you different, aren't you?"

Thutmose and his mother talked for a while, though time did not seem to exist. His mother looked at him. "You need to leave now. I love you," she said.

"Will I see you again?" Thutmose asked.

She looked into his eyes. "Life is about having fun," she

said, "so make sure you do. Don't think about death."

"Mother, where is my father?"

She grasped his hand and squeezed it, and the next thing, he was coughing up sand. Metatron and Michael put their wings away, and pulled him up. The first thing Thutmose noticed was how tall these men were, and they were very familiar. He felt a sharp pain in his stomach which promptly disappeared. He felt very confused and disorientated. Why was he getting out of a hole covered in sand? Why were these strange men helping him? Had he got drunk yet again? He was beginning to think he had a serious problem. He couldn't speak properly and was becoming very loud and unmanageable. "Sleep," said Metatron, and Thutmose fell asleep.

"I can't believe we have had to put him to sleep again," said Michael. "He's never going to know life if we have to carry on like this. Oh, why did we ever create the energy lazuli?"

Metatron frowned. "It won't last. We won't be able to knock him out soon. When we say sleep, he will probably tell us to sod off."

They carried Thutmose back to his house and Jophiel joined them to keep guard at the door.

They tidied up whilst Thutmose slept and tried to come up with a plan to let him know he was a god without destroying him.

Thutmose woke and on seeing the three men in his house, jumped out of bed and wanted to fight. Metatron looked at Thutmose and put up his hand, Michael shook his head. Metatron frowned and sent the thought form, *I'm not going to put him to sleep again.* He turned back to Thutmose. "We are not here to harm you, but we do have some important news.

Please just sit down."

Thutmose would not sit down and stood with his back against the wall. He surveyed the angels distrustfully. "What are you doing in my house? Why was I climbing out of a hole? Is this an illusion? Am I dead?"

"No," said Michael. "You are very much alive, perhaps more alive than you know."

"What does that mean?" ventured Thutmose.

Michael sat down. "Do you know anything about angels?"

"Oh, great, now I've got a priest in my house. So am I dying?"

Michael sighed. "Thutmose, what do you remember before we pulled you from the hole by the pyramids? Think."

Thutmose folded his arms and closed his eyes. "I remember seeing my mother in a dream. We had a discussion, I asked her who my father was." The angels looked at each other, worried for a second. "And then I woke up spitting sand," he said. "After that, nothing."

Metatron looked at Michael. "It's the shock."

Thutmose looked at the angels. "What do you mean, 'it's the shock'?"

Metatron sent a thought form to Michael and Jophiel. They all agreed.

"Look," said Metatron. "Clearly your head needs to sort itself out. You're a bit disorientated having got drunk and fallen down that hole, so rest yourself for the rest of the day and we suggest you go to the pyramid party. Join your friends and relax. You have a long night ahead of you."

They quickly left his house. What did they mean by long night? He went to the door and looked out. There was no one there. "That's it." Thutmose threw his hands in the air.

"Not only am I hearing voices, I'm having discussions with people who don't actually exist. I'm officially mad." He threw himself down on his bed and resolved to see a doctor about his drinking problem. He fell asleep and slept fitfully.

He awoke but didn't feel tired; he wasn't even sure why he had needed to sleep. But later in the day, Thutmose made himself ready for the pyramid party and wore his best finery and jewellery. He could easily have passed for royalty. He set off for the party and noticed that there were candles and torches all over – the light was amazing. There was copious amounts of food and wine and lots of people. Thutmose liked crowds; he could people watch for hours. Some people had already had far too much to drink and he felt the party had been well underway before he got there. He was looking for Snefru, his good friend. They would have quite a night ahead of them, providing his wife had let him out, of course. He wandered around asking if anyone had seen Snefru, but the women were far more interested in Thutmose than him finding his friend. Thutmose continued to look around and then he saw him. He made his way to where Snefru was standing talking to some of the pulling crew. Metatron, Michael and Jophiel were close by and watched.

Thutmose walked over to Snefru and put his hand on his shoulder. "Snefru, my good friend." Snefru turned around and screamed, loudly. As Thutmose put his hand on Snefru the attack on him replayed at speed in his mind. He moved his hand and stood looking at Snefru. The pain and anguish was palpable on Thutmose face.

Snefru began to back away. "It's not possible, it isn't, you were dead."

Thutmose stood still. People around were laughing and

repeating, "Dead?" How could this man be dead? He was here in the crowd. Snefru kept backing away and looking at Thutmose, stumbling and falling, his legs felt like jelly. He pulled himself upright and then he turned and ran. Thutmose took off after him; the angels took off after Thutmose, their disguises getting in the way. They knew they had to get to Thutmose before he got to Snefru.

Thutmose ploughed through the crowd with ease, his focus on Snefru. He was the hunter and Snefru the hunted. Thutmose could smell Snefru's blood in his nostrils and for some reason, it made him run faster and he actually wanted to chase him down. "Oh no," said Michael, "he's feeling the blood rush. We may need to fly and apprehend him before he reaches Snefru."

Snefru ran, pushing things in Thutmose's way. They fell behind him, cluttering the path, but Thutmose jumped over them like hurdles. His head was down and he was angry. The blood was coursing through his veins; he knew now exactly what had happened.

Snefru ran out into the desert and was exhausted. He stopped and he put his hands up. He couldn't breathe. Thutmose stopped and walked towards him like a lion to prey. The angels were close but by the law of God, this was a human error. They were not allowed to intervene. It would be up to Thutmose to deal with this and with the energy imbued him by the angels, they all hoped he would make the right decision. He would be lost should he take after his father.

Thutmose looked at Snefru. "You were my friend. We were together for years, you took me under your wing, you killed me? Why would you kill me?"

Snefru put his hands on his knees and looked at Thutmose

with a laughing smile. "I don't know what you mean. You aren't dead, you are here. I didn't kill you; you are very much alive. What are you talking about?"

Thutmose stood and looked at him. "Why would you hurt me? I was your friend. I wanted to learn from you, you were my teacher, I respected you."

Snefru stood up with his hands on his hips. He had some of his breath back. "Maybe, maybe I was jealous. Maybe I thought you were after my job. You haven't aged, Thutmose, but look at me. Look at my body, my face, my hands. I have few years left in me, you have many. You don't look any different now than you did twenty years ago. How old are you, Thutmose? How old? Why aren't you on your knees like me? Do you have pain when you wake up in the morning? Is every day hard work when you get out of bed? You do not suffer as I do, Thutmose. What is your secret? What is your secret?"

Thutmose looked at Snefru and for a few short seconds felt pity. "I have no secret, Snefru. I have the genes of my father and my mother. I was born to whom I was born to; it was not my fault. I have no secret. All I know is you were my friend and you tried to kill me. Now? Now I will tell people what you have done to me and you will lose everything — your wife, your children, your home. You will be sorry." Thutmose turned his back; the angels breathed a sigh of relief.

Without warning, Snefru drew a dagger from his sandal and threw it towards Thutmose. In a split second Thutmose turned and caught it. Snefru's mouth fell open and he dropped to his knees. Thutmose put the knife on the sandy floor and walked away. The disgust in his eyes crushed Snefru, who hung his head. The angels followed. Michael put his hand on Thutmose's shoulder. "Well done," he said, and they all made their way towards Thutmose's house. The angels knew who was close by but they said nothing and just kept walking.

Still on his knees, Snefru tried to push himself up but he felt a hard hand push him back down. "Oh, don't get up for me," said the voice. Snefru looked up and saw what appeared to be a man complete with horns on his head looking down at him. He was confused. Was this someone in disguise? An act for the party? Then it suddenly dawned on him that whatever this was, it was very real. The scream caught in his throat; the horror stopped him yelling out.

The face suddenly distorted to something indescribably ugly. Snefru couldn't speak; he couldn't tear his eyes away from this abhorrent mask looking at him. But the eyes, the eyes seemed so beautiful, flashing mother of pearl. "What you see in my face is the ugliness of man over thousands and thousands of years," it sneered. "You have all made me this way, you're cruel, you lie, you cheat, you gossip, you are jealous of each other, the whole of the human race is cruel. How can you live with yourselves, when you see what you have done to me?" Snefru whimpered. "You see, when you upset the family of man, you upset gods much higher than you think," it said. Lucifer poked Snefru in his cheek. "Jealousy is such a horrible crime. Your mistake, no, no, your *massive* mistake, was that you attacked my son." Lucifer grinned at Snefru, tilting his head. He whispered in Snefru's ear, "Now call me old fashioned but I always say that Karma will come back and bite you and when it does, well now, it can be quite dreadful, don't you think? Don't answer that, I already know the answer. Yeeesss, I know exactly what you are thinking and I know exactly what you have done. I also know, that had you not killed my son, you were going to volunteer for him to die in the pyramid along with your pulling crew, to guide your Pharaoh to the next life and take his home and property as though it were your own. MY SON!" Lucifer yelled. "Anyway," he continued calmly now, "your friends are waiting for you, both dead of course and both are in Hell. They tried to run, but nothing can outrun me. Seek and ye shall find, and I always, always find."

Snefru was so terrified, his bowels released.

"Your friends are having quite the jolly time in Hell, but keep complaining about the heat. But if you are on fire all the time, I suspect it does get warm. But you? I wanted you to say goodbye to this earth before I take you there, in a special sort of way. You are going to be the main guest of honour." Lucifer bent down and spoke directly to Snefru's face. "Your error of judgement has cost you dear, my friend. I know you have a wife and children and they will suffer because of your stupidity, but to show I am not completely heartless, I will arrange for a new father for them. Your wife has never thought much of you. She has always thought you incompetent and useless and she could hardly bear to have you touch her. She never wanted to marry you, but you know that, don't you? You forced her to anyway by payment of a debt. Sad. So now you will pay your debt. So, big world, without any more ado, Snefru will be coming to our own little party."

Snefru couldn't say anything. He was in shock, his body shaking, he was crying and couldn't speak. His eyes widened as Lucifer dragged him off, then suddenly he began to kick and scream. "Oh yes," said Lucifer. "Fight, please fight, it's so much more fun when you fight." Shoving long bony fingers into Snefru's mouth, he dragged him away and Hell split open. "Hello, everyone!" Lucifer shouted. "Time for a party. I've brought the food and drink."

Screaming and yelling could be heard rising from the pit of the ground and then suddenly, the ground closed behind him and the desert was calm, quiet and peaceful. The moon was high and the stars glistened brightly. The angels looked at each other and cringed.

CHAPTER 10

Thutmose entered his house and sat down. He put his head back and stared at the ceiling. It was painted with stars and goddesses. He looked at the three large men who had followed him home and were in his house. He still wasn't certain who they were, except they seemed to be like bodyguards. He felt tired again, but awake at the same time and his mind was moving very fast from one thing to another. For the last few weeks life had seemed very strange. *Strange?* he thought. *More like weird.* He could not comprehend the gravity of it all. Thutmose stood up and walked to his cabinet. He offered the angels a drink; they politely declined.

Thutmose poured himself one. "You'll have to excuse me drinking alone," he said. "I think I have a drink problem. Funny thing, though, I can't get drunk unless I really want to, and right now… I really, really want to. Would you like to tell me what is going on?"

Michael stood up. "You are not who you think you are," he said. "And you don't have a drink problem. You had, let's say, an unexpected event happen to you and it changed the course of your life."

"What, so am I immortal or something? Is that why I'm not dead?" Thutmose started laughing.

"Yes," said Jophiel.

Michael and Metatron looked at Jophiel and rolled their

eyes and threw their arms up in the air, as though saying, 'We really can't believe you just came out with it.'

Jophiel shrugged and put his hands up as if to say, 'Well someone had to say something,' and was making a face.

Thutmose stopped laughing. "I thought as much," he said.

The angels all looked at one another, then Michael looked at Thutmose. "When did you know?"

"Oh, just before I was killed and put in the hole." The angels looked confused. "I knew there was something different in my late teens," Thutmose continued, "and my dead mother just confirmed it. I fell off a mountainside, when I was a young boy, did you know that? I fell off and didn't hurt myself. My friends were petrified, but I wasn't. Then a friend jumped after me because he thought if I could do it, so could he. He died. I don't bruise longer than a few hours, or sometimes not at all. I don't bleed for longer than a few minutes and my cuts self-heal. As Snefru pointed out, I haven't aged. I did notice that too. I hear voices that belong to people I'm nowhere nearby. I can run as fast as a cat, if not faster..."

"Cat?" said Metatron. Jophiel was behind Thutmose making breast signs and cat ears, meaning to portray Bastet. Thutmose turned around and looked at him. "I know what is happening behind my back. I can move so fast it gives me motion sickness."

"Oh, you'll get over that," said Jophiel, waving his hand and folding his arms.

Thutmose continued, "I can catch moving knives, as you've just witnessed. I dream about bloody angels, I see goddesses when I meditate and now I've survived death, so which of those things do you think might have given it away?" He was shrieking now, his voice rising. "And who the hell are you three?" The angels said nothing. "I can't read your minds because you have blocked me off. Oh yes, I know about that too. Well, actually that's something I only learned in the past ten minutes, which means you have some special sort of ability. Now tell me I'm wrong!"

Michael stood up. "You know that drink you were offering? Well, I think we all need one."

"Good idea," said Jophiel, a little too excitedly.

God was listening in on the conversation. He put his hand to his head. "Oh no," he said.

CHAPTER 11

Thutmose stirred his coffee and looked out onto Paris from his veranda. He remembered the discussion he had with the three large men that night in Cairo. He hadn't seen them since that night and not long after their meeting, he had started to have bad dreams. The dreams were violent and aggressive; there were thunderstorms, people screaming, fire and death, and then suddenly, his dreams would give way to calmness. The old lady in the desert had vanished after his visit; he supposed she had died or moved. Her house hadn't seemed a very permanent place, but he had never been able to get his hands on the tea she had created. Shame, really, because it had been a very calming tea and he fancied it could help him to meditate. He never slept for long though and it didn't affect him either. He had got used to it; in fact he could go for months without sleeping, but it was like recharging a battery when he did sleep.

He had returned to the village of his birth and had been met with hostility. People did not want to talk to him and they were afraid of him. He found one elderly lady in the village who had been a friend of his mother. She lost her breath when he walked into her house. She knew immediately who he was. She was old and infirm and with the help of her daughter she made a sign of Seth and Horus and pointed towards Thutmose. Her daughter was motioning for him to leave. He realised she thought he was evil. He set out to discover the story and asking around the village, it suddenly became clear that the story of his mother's pregnancy was true. The god who had visited her in the night was Lucifer, she had borne the son of the Devil, and it was Thutmose. He was young and vibrant and it was this curse, as he saw it, that had kept him moving over the millennia.

He had become a recluse for years following this revelation and shunned the company of people. As the centuries passed, Cairo changed, people he knew died. He left his home, selling it to a farmer, and he made his way across Europe. The centuries brought him into contact with many leaders, invaders, murderers, painters, ship builders, architects, builders and plumbers, in fact he met people from every walk of life. He always had an opportunity to learn and to pass on his knowledge. He was clever, a quick learner and was never short of money. Over the years, his fortune had grown and now he had more money than the currencies of the countries put together – he was extremely rich. It wasn't just money, there were properties and financial investments. Literally everything he touched turned to gold. He suspected his father had a hand in it somewhere, and he wouldn't be wrong. He had, though, been generous; he had set up charities and given money away easily to worthy causes. Thutmose was by all accounts, a good man.

For a few years, Thutmose employed an accountant who had siphoned off some of Thutmose's money. He thought that Thutmose was so rich, he would never miss a few thousand pounds. Ever righteous, Thutmose had taken the man to court and won. The man had become unemployable and had taken to begging in the streets. One late evening, he broke into Thutmose's home with the intention of stealing anything that would make him a few pounds. He had knowledge of the house, having lived and worked there in a delegated office for years. Watching him from the darkness, Thutmose mused as the man fumbled about his home, then he became uncontrollably angry. Thutmose approached the man and at the last minute, he turned around. Thutmose appeared to have blacked out and had grabbed him by the throat and broken his neck, watching as he fell into a heap on the floor. Rather than panic, Thutmose went into the dark depths of the cellar of his house to obtain tools to dispose of the body. On returning to the library floor, the body was gone. He saw a figure disappear into the darkness; the smell told him it was Lucifer. Curiously, Thutmose felt no remorse. He had in fact done the man a favour, he pondered. No more nights on the streets in the freezing cold and wet. This was of course noted in Heaven. God and the angels were angry. Lucifer was listening. "One-nil Daddy," he laughed.

"He has broken a divine rule and there will be consequences." God walked away.

"The battle begins," said Sandalphon.

After all these centuries, people were still searching for solutions as to how the pyramids were built, how the obelisks were created. What stories Thutmose could tell them. He heard people discussing it and their theories and he listened with interest to the different solutions they came up with. Historians and archaeologists were still searching and pondering the great mystery in the search for the tomb of Alexander the Great. Thutmose smiled wryly. He and

Alexander had sat and talked long into the night with Hephaestion, discussing where he would be entombed. Alexander wanted to rest in peace and not be found. Thus far, their plan had worked. But Thutmose giggled to himself. When Alexander had beaten the Persians, Thutmose had stolen his horse. He returned it, of course, but it took his soldiers five days to find Thutmose and they only found him because he had removed his shield. He had watched them marching past, stopping, scanning the area, setting up camp, then whilst they were asleep, he had removed the shield and stolen the commander's horse along with his sword. All were duly returned. He had taken the horse because Alexander had said that nothing went on that he did not know about. It was a challenge because Thutmose knew it wasn't true, and it was in fact Thutmose who could say that nothing went on that he did not know about. Alexander did not punish Thutmose, because he knew about the night Alexander had been unfaithful to Hephaestion. Thutmose left the camp shortly after.

Thutmose remembered that at first, he had felt excited by the thought of watching the world forever, but as time had gone on, his excitement had waned and he had become bored. The centuries dragged on. He had the opportunity in his lifetime to do and see things that most people would only ever dream of. He had people of both sexes move in and out of his life, but he had never fallen in love. It was, he thought, too dangerous to become too emotionally involved. People recognised his aloofness and even though they put much into the relationship with him, he gave nothing and so found himself alone again.

There had been a very much 'too close for comfort' incident when a lover of Thutmose had stayed over one night. They had become very cold and on trying to pull the blanket back over them in Thutmose's enormous bed, they had discovered that Thutmose had levitated and was in fact sleeping above the mattress, in the air, with the blanket. The lover screamed and Thutmose fell to the floor. Thutmose had broken his arm and if that wasn't bad enough, the lover had fallen over in their haste to leave the room, slipped and banged their head on a cabinet, knocking them out cold. However, this worked in Thutmose's favour because he convinced them they had seen his levitation in a dream and fell over when sleep walking. They went their separate ways.

On invading the lover's mind, Thutmose discovered that they thought he was evil, which Thutmose really hated, and they wanted to be as far away from him as possible. Other lovers had been with him for his money, his looks, whatever he was able to offer them rather than what they could give. Sometimes it was because of his status and sometimes just camaraderie. That was the benefit of being able to read people's minds; they couldn't hide anything. Even if Thutmose resolved not to read someone's mind, he always gave in to the temptation and flicked through it like a well-read book.

Finishing his coffee, Thutmose pondered on who the three men had said they were. Strangely enough, he could not read their minds. He did not know if they were gods, but he supposed it were possible. They may be long dead by now, and he envied them; he was ready to become a star constellation in the sky. He knew becoming a star constellation wasn't true, but it was one of the few Egyptian things he liked to hang on to. He felt very lost these days. He desperately wanted to go home but he really needed to speak to Lucifer about how to end this existence he seemed to be stuck in. He walked past his enormous library bookshelves; nearly half of the books were about Egypt. He remembered he had tried to put a stop to Howard Carter invading King Tutankhamen's tomb, but the Egyptian Government had said it was for the good of historical knowledge. He could have fought it and probably won, but he decided that if that was how humans learned, then he would allow them their research. He disapproved highly of the excavation of the bodies and when the Cairo museum had closed, he went inside, made the guards sleep and performed a ritual for the souls. He watched as the spirits rose through the ceiling. Their relief was felt by Thutmose bone deep. He had not been able to remove the curses though. Despite years of reading and practice, curses remained. He had never been able to figure out why. He had no idea that the curses had come from Lucifer. All his curses stuck like super glue; once applied, there was no getting rid of them.

One night, Thutmose cried himself to sleep having prayed to the gods to help him leave the Earth plane. During his sleep, Archangel Raphaël came to his bedside. "Thutmose, stop tormenting yourself. There is so much you can do for mankind. You have been blessed as a god and given a long life. Use it to your advantage, do good deeds and the time will fly. Maybe then, God will look kindly on you and give you the peace you seek. In the meantime, take this gift and run with it. We are watching always."

When Raphael had gone, Thutmose opened his eyes. He knew someone had been in his room. He rose, dressed and made his way towards the centre of Paris. He would wander through the back streets and watch as the world went by. As he walked suddenly there was the smell. "Dad," he said, and he began to run, following the smell like a bloodhound. He had questions that he wanted to ask his father, but no matter how close he came to catching up with him, he never got quite close enough. Lucifer always managed to stay one step ahead.

Lucifer was in a high-rise block of offices, and had come for the soul of a man who was selfish, full of pride and had been particularly evil over his short life span. Lucifer was beginning to panic because he sensed Thutmose was on his way. He was trying desperately to get the person he had come for to admit his crime. "So, admit it," said Lucifer. "Vous avez pris l'argent des vieilles dames, et ne lui en avez pas laissé pour s'occuper." Lucifer was looking out of the office block window and could see Thutmose running down the quayside. The man would not admit his crime and Lucifer was getting very frustrated. "Just admit it, you pig," said Lucifer. The man looked at him in confusion, Lucifer rolled his eyes. "Admets le, cochon." The man still would not admit to his crime and Thutmose was on his way up in the lift so as not to attract attention to himself. Flying up the side of a building like spiderman, because you can, doesn't always mean you should and definitely does not impress. He had been shot at above once by police and the army alike. "Oh for goodness' sake," said Lucifer. "Look, I don't care if you understand me or not. I'm the Devil, I've come for your soul, you're a liar, you did the crime, time's up, we're out of here." He grabbed the man and jumped out of the window with him.

Lucifer created a split in the veil between the worlds, extracted the soul and dropped the body on the quayside, just as Thutmose got into the room.

"Damn, he's fast," said Thutmose. He looked out of the window. "Ewwww, and messy."

Thutmose knew he needed to get out of there before someone accused him of the crime of murder. They would instead think it was suicide, because the man was in fact guilty and once they had researched the records he kept, they would know this. Thutmose could not walk back down the corridor, because people were on their way and would think he was implicated. He jumped out of the window, landing at various points, and made his way back home. People came running towards the room having heard the crash. He heard the echoes of screams as people looked out of the window at the body on the hard concrete ground outside. He was once again disappointed that he didn't meet with Lucifer and he had absolutely no idea why he kept leaving. He would have thought that if a father knew his son wanted to speak to him, he would give him the time. There were so many questions he wanted to ask and so many things he needed to know.

CHAPTER 12

Lucifer was getting really tired of the spell the witch had put on him. He needed to speak to her to get it removed; they had to come to some sort of compromise. It was getting increasingly annoying having people know who you were just as you were about to extract their souls. He knew God wouldn't remove the spell, even though he could, and even though he said that Lucifer was useful for keeping mankind in check. Lucifer would need to speak to Iside and end this battle once and for all, in the best possible way. If she had helped his son, surely she was in forgiveness mode?

Iside knew that Lucifer was looking for her and she was prepared. For two hundred years she had been trapped in ice in a parallel because of his need to extract her energy. She knew he had little time left and this time she was ready. She had just about every spell, every piece of knowledge that she could possibly pull together that had been used over the millennia to keep the Devil at bay. She sat and waited. The ground was vibrating; he was on his way.

Iside sat very still and as Lucifer approached, she put a freeze spell out. His wings were out; he had loosened them because he thought it a possibility she might fire a bolt or arrows at him and he would need to ascend quickly. He wasn't expecting the ice. "Oh, bloody hell," he sighed. The closer he got to Iside's shield, the more frozen his wings became. "Iside!" he shouted. "We need to talk."

"Go away, Lucifer!" she shouted back. "I swear I will shatter you into little pieces and boil you."

Lucifer rolled his eyes. "Seriously, and how long do you think that would last?"

"Do you want to find out?" she shouted.

"I can't do my job if people know who I am. They have a defence set up before I even get to them. Do you know how many bad people that is leaving in the world?" Lucifer gritted his teeth.

"HMMMM, seems to me you are just trying to get back on the good side of God. You don't care about good or bad, you are just a self-serving little snot."

Lucifer was getting angry and the heat from his anger was beginning to melt the ice. Iside knew he could be inside her shield at any moment but she carried on with the spell.

"Iside, we were friends once. Please, please can you release me from this spell? I need to be able to do my job and to be able to move from one place to another quickly." Lucifer was getting truly agitated.

"Friends," Iside said. "Friends? We were more than friends, Lucifer, and all you were interested in was extracting my energy to prolong your time. Well, guess what? When it's over, it's over and you, my ex-friend, are going to be so over."

Lucifer began to breathe very heavily. "Iside, I am trying my best to sort this issue out." He was breathing heavier. "Please, just take the spell off, and there will be no more said."

Iside watched from inside the shield. "You do know I can see you, don't you?" she queried.

"Yes, I know," snapped Lucifer.

"Then go away, Lucifer, and leave quickly… on your skateboard," Iside laughed, "and if you don't go now, you will never hear from me again and people will always know who you are the minute you confront them."

Lucifer let out an almighty roar and exploded with rage turning… into a clown with a daisy on his head. "What the…?" Lucifer couldn't believe it and Iside was laughing so much she fell off her seat. "A clown. You think I'm a clown?? You really have gone too far, Iside." Lucifer put his head down and started to recite the reveal spells of old. Iside sat still. She thought this might happen and as fast as Lucifer recited the reveal spell, she was reciting the conceal spell. The shield was flashing backwards and forwards. Each time it moved, Lucifer stepped forward, then Iside moved it one step back. He could see her, then he could not see her. This went on for hours; both Lucifer and Iside were getting tired.

Lucifer stopped. He sat on the floor and folded his wings. "Iside, wherever you go, I will follow you, I will find you."

"You're just an arrogant pig, Lucifer," said Iside. "You could have killed me."

"But I didn't, did I?" he sighed.

"Because Bastet stopped you? You always drive people away, Lucifer, you had a wonderful home and what did you do? You tried to destroy your father. You were seeking anyone and anything that could give you extra time and you just didn't care about the consequences."

Lucifer started to write in the sand. "You took care of my son," said Lucifer. "Do you know he nearly died?"

"Don't play the sympathy card," said Iside. "He didn't nearly die, he's a god, for goodness' sake, except he doesn't do anything with his gifts, he just mourns the fact he is still alive. You could take all *his* energy if you really wanted to. Once that happened no one would dare touch you."

"Except God," reflected Lucifer, "and anyway, I don't want to harm him like that."

"You're a liar, Lucifer," said Iside. "You would have had him work for you as a demon if Michael and Metatron hadn't intervened. You even pushed Michael away from you."

"No," said Lucifer, "he just chose the wrong side."

"Looks like the right from where I'm sitting," said Iside.

Lucifer continued to write in the sand. Iside couldn't see what he was writing but suddenly her shield began to shake. Lucifer stood up. He shook his wings free of the sand. "You see, Iside, no one trusts me anymore, but when they want something bad to happen to someone, what do they do? They read the blackest books, they make the darkest wishes and they yell the hardest spells, and do you know who has created all those things for people to use, watching over them as they do it and helping them to do it? It's me, Iside. Me, me, me, me, me. They all come to me, and all I ask in return is love. Do they give it to me? No, on their death beds who do they reject knowing? ME! Who do they cry for? It's BLOODY HIM!" Lucifer shrieked, pointing upwards.

Lucifer stomped about and banged his feet on the floor and screamed with rage. He stormed towards Iside, running at speed, and crashed through her shield. He was panting with rage.

"But I know spells no one else knows, Iside, because I bloody created every one of them and so..." he panted, "so here I am, Iside. Whilst you were telling me how awful I was, I was writing old spells in the sand. Now remove this bloody spell before I eat you!"

Iside stood up and threw hot tar all over Lucifer. His wings stuck like glue and they pinned themselves to his body. Iside moved away and began to pray. "Oh, bloody hell," said Lucifer. He turned around and began to walk away.

Iside stopped praying. "Where are you going?" she shouted.

"I've had enough," said Lucifer. "You know what? I don't care how many people are going bad on this earth – you can all deal with them. I'm going home and I will stay there until I pass into oblivion, but you explain to my father that he has an extra job on his hands because you ruined everything." Lucifer skulked off towards the desert and split the door to Hell open. He started to walk downwards.

"Lucifer!" shouted Iside.

"Get lost," he said, and carried on walking. "I have to use a bloody skateboard for speed because of you. Just leave me alone, and have you any idea how difficult it is to get tar off your wings? I have to use a special cleaner and it stinks, I stink bad enough already." He folded his arms and kept walking.

"Lucifer!" shouted Iside.

"I said get lost!" shouted Lucifer. "Are you deaf?"

"No, I heard you… Lucifer… Lucifer…" But he closed the gate behind him. "Oh dear," said Iside. "I think I've really done it now."

Lucifer was really smarting from the argument he had just had with Iside, but being the King of Deceit, he was biding his time. He had to stop her saying the prayer; it could have transported him to any dimension and it would have taken him hours to find his way back, even days or years if she had repeated it. She would have been gone by the time he returned. Her shields would be up and it could have taken him years to find her again. He only knew where she was this time because one of the gods let the witch out of the bag. If he killed Iside the spell would be removed instantaneously and he would owe her nothing. However, then there would be the problem with the rest of the gods; they would all be out to eradicate him. Unfortunately, Iside was a popular god and he really didn't fancy having problems for eternity.

Lucifer made his way back up to the Earth plane and shouted to Iside. She stayed silent and watched him from a distance. He was certain she was still close by. Iside knew Lucifer would be much less dangerous with his wings exposed, so she waited for him to shake them loose. There was more angel than devil with his wings unprotected. She could remove the tar for him, but he could do that himself, he was the Devil for goodness' sake, but she would need to get quite close and that was risky. She put her spell stone necklace around her neck. If push came to shove, she would snap it off and throw it, it would be her last chance at getting away.

She removed her shield. "Lucifer…" He turned around. "If you attempt anything, I will leave you in your current state."

Lucifer raised his arms. "I know," he said. "I'm not that stupid." They walked towards each other. He knelt down, she was caught off guard. "I'm sorry, Iside. I am an arrogant angel who has lost his way but I cannot do anything about that now; it's engrained into my very nature. My father has disowned me and I am trying, and failing it would seem, to make my way in this GOD FORSAKEN WORLD." He exaggerated the words, looking at the sky. "And making dreadful mistakes along the way. I ask you, as the angel I once was, to please forgive me…" Lucifer changed into the angel of light.

"You are so beautiful, Lucifer," said Iside. "Why couldn't you remain with your father and be this angel?"

He smiled. "Because..." he said, "I am foolish and arrogant... I am sorry for the pain I caused you and the agony you endured for 200 years. It was selfish of me. I cannot begin to imagine what you felt and the disappointment you must have felt in me. I am sorry."

Iside looked at Lucifer and told him to stand up. Iside began to glow all the colours of the spectrum. She was incredibly beautiful; her long, dark hair was dancing in joyfulness of the colours that surrounded her. She held Lucifer's hands and recited the spell of correction and no harm. She called on the gods to help her to remove the infliction on Lucifer and stated that henceforth, no one who had done wrong and was deserving of Hell, would know Lucifer by sight, sound, sense, or smell, unless he decided that it was so. She used energy imbued within her to remove the tar from his wings and prayed that he would be protected from all further spells and harm until the end of his time unless he provoked her.

The winds swirled and the sand spun in small tornadoes. Lighting cracked and touched its fingers around them. Then as quickly as it had arisen, it settled. Lucifer felt a sense of power course through him that he had felt had been missing. He held Iside's hands and thanked her. She smiled, looking into those beautiful mother of pearl eyes. He was so beautiful. Then she saw the eyes of the snake and they flashed red. Before she could pull away, Lucifer quickly spun her around, ripped off her stone necklace and broke her neck. She fell to the floor and he dusted off his hands. He knew she would recover but it could take many, many years. He hadn't killed her and anyway, he wasn't really bothered what the other gods thought; he could look after himself. He didn't care about being selfish and arrogant, it was a nice little quirk to his attractive personality. Not many gods wanted to take on the dragon, especially as he could become very dangerous and destructive. He walked away with a spring in his step, leaving Iside in the sand. He neither cared who nor what found her. She had caused him problems for longer than she had been in a coma from his attempted energy drain of her. Then he stopped walking and looked back. It was too easy and too tempting. He strode meaningfully back towards her, and whispered in her ear, "Oh, foolish witch to take the Devil for a fool. I am the King of Deceit and you, you were so very easy to deceive. Oh, look into my beautiful eyes, Iside." He picked up her body and looked directly into her eyes. He knew she could still see him, and he concentrated with his full energy and drained hers. Each drain gave him an extra buzz, but when he drained Thutmose, he would be almost invincible.

Lucifer dropped her body onto the floor like a sack of stones. He started to laugh. He spun, he danced, he cartwheeled, his excitement could be felt throughout the spirit realm. The twelve angels looked at each other and looked towards God. God held their gaze for just a second then turned and walked away. There was nothing he wanted to do… yet. He knew the depths of Lucifer, and he could not let this pass without some type of recrimination, but it needed to be fair.

Lucifer flew as the dragon, twirling, spinning, gliding, then ploughed through the gates of Hell as himself, laughing as life in the desert exploded around him. Once he had disappeared

Michael and Geb appeared on the sand next to Iside. They saw how it had aged her; she was close to the equivalent of death of a human. Geb picked up her skinny, limp body hanging like a dead branch on a tree. "Leave her to me, Michael," he said. Michael nodded. He watched as Geb walked off into the desert and disappeared. Michael looked into the empty space that had held Lucifer. Michael's sadness was palpable. Sometimes he thought there was hope for Lucifer; today, he realised there was none. He ran and flew, his tears mixed with the kaleidoscopic multicoloured fluorescence of his wings.

Thutmose wandered about his home, admiring all the acquisitions he had collected over the years. Museums and collectors would never be able to obtain such things. Some of the things he had, museums were still searching for and some they didn't even know existed or were considered to be mythical. He walked into his dining room and in the corner stood a very old, but very secure safe. It resembled a large, old, beautiful and intricately decorated wooden cabinet, with horses, gods, nymphs and trees. It had been given to him in the 17th century by an elderly woman who had been, shall we say, grateful, for the attention that he had bestowed on her. For him, it was curiosity; she was a curio. What would it be like to impart his knowledge of the various things he had learned about sex, love and passion over the millennia, to a much older woman? For her, it was her last chance to feel the passion ignited in her before she became too old for any sort of male attention.

It was a very old and expensive item and only three of them existed, that were known of. The old lady knew there was something different about Thutmose. He told her his name was Joseph, and she wanted to give him something to remember her by. "It's in case you have something secret that you don't want anyone to know about." She winked. He loaded the cabinet onto his horse and cart himself. She marvelled at his strength, but to him, it was as light as a feather. He thanked her and rode away. He knew he would never see her again, and she knew too. Still, she didn't cry or create a fuss, she just held onto the memories of 'Joseph' until she passed on, twenty years later. It was then that he discovered she had left her mansion to him. She had no children, and he had made her happy, so it never raised any eyebrows. He didn't move into it, though, because his continual youthful looks would have raised questions. He sold it in the years to come, for far more than it was ever built for. He took nothing from it; all the items remained intact, and it eventually became a museum, and a town grew up around it. But he held on to the cabinet. It wasn't for sentimental reasons, it was because of its value, beauty and security. He approached it now with exhilaration. What he wanted was tucked away inside.

There was an old legend which had grown over the centuries and had its roots in Egypt. It told the story of a man who had uncovered a diamond created by angels, and it had given him the knowledge of foresight and youth. The man had used the diamond for evil deeds; he laid waste to towns and cities throughout the known world. He had grown rich on the property of others and created disease and illness. The man and the diamond eventually disappeared, but it was said that one day he would return. When Thutmose had first heard of this legend, he had laughed until he cried. It was all nonsense and any wasting of towns and cities had been down to nature or, and he hated to think about it, his father and the intervention of war. However, now he was smiling as with each turn of the locks on the cabinet, with each slide of a latch, with each movement made of gold, inside the little doors that moved with the solid gold keys, which had to be put in to the locks in a certain sequence, he was getting closer and closer to the fabled diamond. Of course, it wasn't a diamond, it was the Lapis Lazuli that he had found; the same piece that had made him immortal, the same piece that would now help him to draw his father to him. He would, even if it killed him, make his father speak to him and tell him why he had been avoiding him for all this time. He opened the final secret door and there it was. Glowing as brightly and as beautiful as the very day it had entranced him, he touched it with his fingers and drew it out of its silken sheath. He remembered when he had woken in the desert, after the strange dream. He wondered how it was that he had managed to hold on to it. Especially if he had been so very drunk.

He turned and walked to his huge rugged bookcase, which he had built into the walls of his home. He laid his hand on the bookcase and it opened, closing softly behind him as he made his way along a stone corridor lit by flamed torches. He used the torches as it reminded him of Cairo and the nights in the desert that he had enjoyed so much. Each one lit up as he passed, the flames jumping to life. He never questioned how or why this happened. He made his way to a stone altar, surrounded by crystals, candles and statues. He would begin the rituals of old and draw his father to him. Unknown to Thutmose, something had been watching from outside. The Lapis Lazuli had rung out when it was removed from the cabinet, and the sound although unheard by humans, hit the heavens with a long sounding '*dong*'.

"The thieving little…" said Michael.

"We haven't seen Thutmose in a while," Jophiel reflected. "I think we should pay him a visit."

Michael frowned. "Are you suggesting that we go and rob him?"

"Au contraire," said Jophiel, "I suggest we persuade him to hand it back. It can't do anything for him now, but it can cause lots of trouble if we let him play with it."

They agreed to visit him, but would not fly.

The eyes of the dwarves were watching intently through the window of Thutmose home. They had seen the Lapis. They looked at each other and nodded. They huddled together and slipped through the veil into Lucifer's kingdom. "He has it," said the lead dwarf, Gumbod. "He went through a hole in his wall and took it with him. It is glowing as bright as a star."

Lucifer stood up, pulling his tail with him as though it were a long robe. "Well, I need it, but I can't get it myself, someone is going to have to get it for me, and we need to get to it before the angels and gods get to it first. Get a team together and bring it back. If he follows you, lose him. I want the Lapis, not Thutmose… yet. If God saw him coming here, he would blame me and we would all be eradicated."

The Lapis was no longer functional as an immortal life-giving item, but it did hold the secrets of how it was created, and it held secrets of the universe.

The dwarves turned and ran as fast as they could, making absolutely no noise whatsoever. They slipped back through the veil and onto the earth, outside of Thutmose's home. Thutmose was reciting the old spells, candles were flickering, the stones seemed to take on a life of their own. They moved and writhed like loose mud. His statues seemed to move and beckon him forward. His voice grew louder and a wind began to blow, then with one powerful blast of energy, the house shook, the ground beneath Thutmose's feet shivered and before him stood… Seth. Seth looked slightly perplexed to say the least. He stood and stared at Thutmose. "What the hell have you done?" Seth looked around himself and looked down at his legs, which were missing. "Oh, this is just peachy," said Seth.

Thutmose looked confused. "What are you doing here and what are you doing in my ritual? I was chasing my father."

Seth threw his hands in the air. "Bloody beginners, you all do it. You don't read the small print, do you? I'm obviously not your father and you've obviously done the spell wrong. Are you illiterate? Can you read?" he asked very sarcastically. "Give me the book you were using."

Thutmose looked uncomfortable. "I, em, don't have a book, I've remembered it by heart." He grew more uncomfortable as Seth grew angrier.

"You've remembered it by heart? You've remembered nothing. Have you any idea where you just dragged me away from? Have you any idea that gods can live in an alternative universe and have as much fun as they want?" Then Seth stopped. He squinted and walked towards Thutmose. Thutmose was shaking slightly and it was obvious there was something emitting from his being, but he stood his ground as Seth started towards him. He towered over Thutmose and slowly bent down. He got close to him and began to sniff him. "Well, well, who do we have here?" Thutmose was quiet. "I know who you are," said Seth, and just as he was about to say it, he was hit in the face with a furry black ball. It knocked him backwards and he landed on his back. He was enraged. He jumped up with a roar that echoed around the walls and back again, and attacked the two little black balls that were attacking Thutmose. Grabbing hold of them with huge spade-like hands, he promptly ate them.

The room became filled with lots of little black balls whizzing all over the place and clearly looking for something. They were bouncing off the walls, hitting Thutmose in the stomach and knocking him over. Seth was eating the little black balls as fast as he could catch them. Thutmose managed to stagger towards his altar where he grabbed the Lapis and swallowed it. The little black balls stopped; only then did it become obvious what they were. They were Lucifer's dwarves. They looked at Thutmose, horrified. "He swallowed it," said one of the dwarves. "We'll have to take him with us."

Gumbod walked forward. "No, we can't take him with us, we'd be eradicated." Then he turned and saw Seth. Gumbod froze on the spot.

"Well," said Seth, "I thought this was going to be my unlucky day, but by chance, it's turned into a lucky day. Hello, you thieving little scarab. Come here." He grabbed for Gumbod, who fled and ran as fast as his short little legs would carry him, with the other dwarves in pursuit.

"Why are we running?" said one of the dwarves. "There are more of us than them."

"Because," said Gumbod, "Lucifer only threatens to eat you, but Seth really does… Where are the basketball team?" They all screamed and took flight back into Thutmose's garden and disappeared through the veil. It was better to be chastised and beaten by Lucifer than eaten by Seth. Six of their best basketball players had just been eaten; they were bound to lose this year.

Seth turned and smiled at Thutmose. "Let me shake your hand," said Seth. "I wondered when I would meet you. We had all heard Lucifer had a son, but you weren't supposed to last so long, no offence."

"None taken," said Thutmose.

"I apologise for telling you off about the spell thing," said Seth, "but when you have a beginner who calls the God of death, I always end up at their altar and they usually don't know why they have called you, or have tried it just to scare themselves and their friends. I am not usually minus my legs, but there's a first time for everything."

"I'm not actually a beginner," said Thutmose. "I've done it before, and last time, I ended up with Neith. Have you ever tried to stop a cow, who is really annoyed, from shitting on your carpet? Truth be known, I actually don't want to be here, to be honest, it's been fun but I'm really ready to leave now."

Seth put his hand on Thutmose's shoulder. "Listen, my friend, there's a sort of rule, like a policy, really, terms and conditions, that type of thing, rules you have to live by. I know how you can leave this life, but I'm not supposed to tell you. It's down to family members, so I guess I know why you are chasing Lucifer. There is more to being immortal than being saintly all the time. Come and have some fun. I know *you* can't get me back from whence I came, but fortunately, I can and I can get you back from where we are going. Come and see what we get up to on the other planes and if you really want out, then I guess you are just going to have to find your dad in your own time. He's a slippery bugger, your father." Seth opened a portal and walked through it. "Are you coming?" Thutmose held back. "Oh, come on, even if just for five minutes?"

"Five minutes?" repeated Thutmose. Seth nodded. Thutmose stepped through the portal.

"By the way…" said Seth, "does your dad still have his skateboard?"

Thutmose said, "Skateboard?" then the portal closed.

CHAPTER 14

On returning to his home from the party with the gods, Thutmose just about made it to his bed to sleep. Whilst sleeping he began to dream. An avalanche of dramas and pictures filled his dreams, cascading through his mind like an unstoppable waterfall. He was seeing things he had never seen before, at least he didn't think he had. There were angels, dwarves, caves, ice melting and freezing, fire, vast golden courts, armies of creatures partying. There were darker things, darker shadows, clouds, mountains, burning pathways, burning cities, people seemingly lost forever in a bottomless pit. He noticed that in the dreams, people seemed to be able to see him, talk to him, ask for help. There were giants, he dreamt of Sodom and Gomorrah, and an almighty explosion which suddenly woke him. He remembered he had swallowed the Lapis and needed to retrieve it. He sat on a cushion in the middle of his living room and surrounded himself with light and images of the Lapis. He cupped his hands in front of him and relaxed, his images of the Lapis getting brighter and brighter. He opened his eyes and there it was in his hands. He decided to put it away and try at some other time to get to his father.

It was noon. He wandered out to his veranda and sat down, looking out over the city.

Life for him had become much quieter now, but how he

wished he had not wasted so many millennia desperately seeking his purpose. Looking out over the horizon, he suddenly saw it. He could just see it on the edge of a roof. It was faint, but yes, it was definitely there. A deep orange line, almost like someone had drawn with a crayon around a roof. Perhaps it was the sun, but there was too much cloud for the sun to break through with any type of shaft of light. The colour bounced; he kept looking, but it kept rising in little waves. It shot upwards, then back down and seemed to glow on the edge of the rooftops. There was definitely something there. It was moving slowly towards him. Was it going to cover the city? He didn't know. He kept looking, and as he was looking, the stratosphere became very silent. There was undeniably no noise. He stood up and walked to the edge of his balcony and looked over to the city below. It was unquestionably still. Nothing moved, nothing. No cars, no people, no animals, it was absolutely completely still. He kept watching. The cloud was getting closer but he didn't move, he wasn't afraid. He knew whatever was in that cloud, wanted him, he could feel it, and he was ready to meet it head on. It paused its movement for a few seconds, then reaching his balcony, it started to disperse, and life as usual carried on below. He was not surprised when the three men he had met in Cairo stepped out of nowhere and onto the veranda floor. "Hello, Thutmose," they smiled.

"My friends," he laughed. "Such a long time. Where have you been?"

"So, what have you been up to?" said Jophiel.

"Well, I could tell you, but I think you already know?"

They all chatted idly for a while, then Thutmose said, "So, why are you here? You have made this journey and a pretty dramatic entrance for a purpose. What is it?"

"Well, we have come to retrieve the Lapis."

"What Lapis?" Thutmose frowned.

Michael walked over to the secret cabinet. "The one that is in this drawer."

Thutmose shrugged his shoulders... "I'm not sure what you mean." Michael smiled, and holding out his hand, the Lapis emerged through the cabinet and into his hand. Thutmose looked suitably ashamed. "Oh, that Lapis?"

"It belongs to us." Metatron laughed. "So it will come when we call it."

There was a moment of awkwardness then Thutmose said, "Seriously, why are you here? You could have come into my house at any time and retrieved the Lapis. What's happening?"

"There's going to be a battle for you and your very soul," said Jophiel.

"Flipping heck, Jophiel! Don't just come out with it, you have to prepare your receiver for these things!" Michael said.

Jophiel shrugged. "Doesn't matter how you say it, it'll still mean the same thing, and anyway, it's my thing, it's what I do."

Michael looked at Thutmose, and quietly repeated, "There's going to be a pretty big battle, and you will be at the centre of it. We need as much help as we can get and it will take place in Abu Simbel. We will be battling for you, and your very life and soul will depend on the outcome. As mighty as we are, we cannot afford to lose this battle. There will, as the humans say, be Armageddon if we do. We need anyone and everyone who is prepared to fight on our side."

"And that's the way you do it!" said Jophiel, raising his arms up in the air.

Thutmose sat down. "I think I've always known that something like this would happen, but who are you, really? And why now? Why do you need help?"

Metatron folded his arms and gave a little squint. "Have you ever read the books of Enoch?" Thutmose looked at him quizzically. "Didn't think so," said Metatron. "You people would learn so much more if you bothered to read the books. What have you been reading over the millennia? Never mind, don't answer that, it was obviously not Enoch."

"Mez." Michael frowned.

"Look, Thutmose," said Metatron, "you know who your dad is, right? Well, let's just say that your dad doesn't really have the smartest of personalities and he can be really mean sometimes. He was the first born in Heaven and God made him absolutely perfect, in every single way. Anyway, Luci… er, Lucifer, got a little bit too big for his boots and decided to try to overthrow our father. Our father was really angry…"

"Really angry?" said Jophiel. "Bloody ballistic, more like."

"Our father… who art in Heaven," Metatron grinned a little… "became very angry and Michael and the rest of us threw your dad out of Heaven with all the other angels who joined him. The Watchers were watching the women on Earth and decided to get together with them…"

"Fornicate…" said Jophiel.

Michael sighed… "Then they created babies who grew into giants and it was down bank from there. So, anyway, in the midst of all the tantrums, your father decided that he needed a child on Earth to take over where he left off, just in case everything should go belly up, and seeing how beautiful and virtuous your mother was, he transformed himself into your mother's husband and you are it. You were meant to be here to create Hell on Earth. He did not foresee that our father would intervene in the way that he did, and stop his plan."

Thutmose didn't respond and looked like someone had just slapped his face. Jophiel waved his hand in front of his eyes. "Helloooooooo, hellooooooooooo? Thutmose, are you in there?"

Thutmose looked up very slowly. "You're older than me? You've been here since the world began…?"

"Well, yes…" said Michael.

"So, you aren't just gods, are you?"

"Well, no, we're… Look, Thutmose, are you OK? We thought you might have sussed it by now."

Thutmose began little hiccup noises and little breaths. "Oh my… Oh my… Oh my… Oh my…"

"Oh shit," said Jophiel. He's going into meltdown…"

"Oh… my."

"Thutmose stop it," said Michael. "Just calm down… sleep…" Nothing happened.

"He's too old for the baby talk," reflected Metatron. "Once they start ageing, you can't do anything with them, they're a bit like humans that way."

Thutmose started to hyperventilate…

"We're killing him," said Jophiel, hands waving and his wings emerged and began flapping very fast.

"We aren't killing him, he's a god, just waft him with your wings," said Michael. "Fresh air might help." Jophiel moved closer. Thutmose panicked and his eyes grew even wider. He climbed onto the back of his chair and fell off.

"This isn't going well…" said Jophiel.

"Oh, you think?" said Metatron, and when they moved to

the back of his chair, Thutmose was gone. "Where is he?" said Metatron. They all stood very quietly and could hear him breathing. "He's close…"

Then as if by magic, he appeared exactly where he fell.

"He's asleep," said Michael.

"No he isn't," said Metatron. "I think he is in shock. We had best sit him up again."

"Why didn't he know we were angels? He's surely had enough weird stuff happen in his life to know we were just slightly different."

"He's never seen our wings out," said Michael thoughtfully, "and we've only ever told him about Lucifer."

"Perhaps he thought we were Chasing the Devil?" said Jophiel. "You know, like some sort of cultists?"

"Well, whatever it was he thought, he had best get over it," said Metatron. "We need him and we need everyone and anyone he knows, from other realms, to help us. This is going to be one hell of a battle. Lift him up."

Pulling him up, Thutmose opened his eyes and appeared much calmer. "Thank you, thank you." he said. "I think you saved my life."

"Saved your life?" asked Jophiel.

"Yes, I was choking on an olive pip. I tried to stand up but you wafted your wings and knocked me off my chair. When I fell on my back, the pip popped out."

The angels looked at each other and burst out laughing. "We thought we were killing you and you were dying of shock because you didn't know who we were."

Thutmose looked slightly embarrassed. "Well I didn't know, but I made a random guess that you are angels? You have been around longer than me and you can travel and make time stop, so I'm guessing I was probably right. Oh, and you have wings."

Metatron smiled. "Yes, huge giveaway, isn't it? Well, that makes things a whole lot easier. We can start making plans. Incidentally, the disappearing is a pretty neat trick."

"Yes, I can do it at will. I've never had it happen by accident before. Bit odd, really, not sure why it happened," pondered Thutmose.

Metatron sat down and studied Thutmose. "You've been on your own a long time?" Thutmose looked uncomfortable. "You've tried to live a human life, but you couldn't, because you simply aren't human. Being alone for thousands of years isn't virtuous, it's ludicrous. You weren't meant to be alone. You haven't changed and that is your undoing. You have not related to the modern world you have tried so hard to fit into, instead, you have remained static. You are the same person who lived and worked in ancient Egypt."

Thutmose played with the end of his plait; it was a habit he had got into when he was nervous. The angels sat down and for the first time in over two thousand years, Thutmose spoke about his hopes, his dreams, his wishes, his experiences and finally, his unwavering desire to leave the earth and finally have some peace. They spoke long into the night and none of them noticed when the night time had come, and passed, and a new day had begun and night had once again, begun to fall.

Eventually, they fell silent. Metatron walked out onto the veranda and looking up into the heavens, closed his eyes. "Is he asleep?" asked Thutmose.

"No, he's talking to our father," said Michael. "We never sleep."

Metatron returned and told Thutmose to pack a bag; he

was going on a journey.

"Where to?"

Metatron smiled broadly. "Abu Simbel."

The excitement on Thutmose face shone. In the darkness outside there were eyes watching. They were red, fiery, and angry.

CHAPTER 15

Thutmose rode with Jophiel. The angels were accompanied by Sandalphon, Raguel and Ariel. Each had been assigned to teach Thutmose a skill and to show him who he really was. When they reached Abu Simbel, the angels watched as Thutmose walked up to the ancient monument. They gave him this time, because they had known this moment would come. Thutmose stood and looked at the very glory of Abu Simbel and his soul connected instantly. He remembered his time here, the happiness he had felt. He walked over to the statues and laid his hands on them and bent his head forward. He closed his eyes, and then without warning, he fell to his knees on the sand, and the tears of millennia began to flow. He had so longed to return to Egypt, his home, where his very soul, throughout the thousands of years, had wished to reside. His body was racked with sobbing and it shook violently with each breath he took. He wept for the family he had lost, he wept for the life he had lost, he wept for the people of Egypt who he had known and the generations of children he no longer knew. He wept because he was no longer human and felt he had been robbed of the chance to become a father, a lover, a person who had lived a normal life, and he cried because he could not die. He threw back his head, crying to the sky. He began praying in Egyptian and the tears fell heavier. Ra was listening with Maat and they viewed him; their tears fell as they felt the pain in this Egyptian who desperately wanted to come home. Thutmose shouted to God to please help him find peace. His soul needed to rest. He was sorry for what had happened, he didn't know what he was doing. The angels knelt and joined in his prayers.

From out of the desert night, walked Geb and Seth. They stood in the shadows, feeling the very depth of sorrow in Thutmose's soul. Thutmose shouted to the Egyptian gods to forgive him for the empty life he had lived and for his lack of understanding, for his greed and his selfishness, for not noticing the many gifts that had been offered to him during his life. He had dreamt of the ghosts of his dreams walking away into the desert in sorrow, unfulfilled and latent. The angels waited patiently. Thutmose dug his hands into the sand and pulled his full hands back to his chest and his heart, moving it over his head and his hair. Rocking backwards and forwards and in complete exhaustion, eventually, the tears stopped, the sobbing subsided, he fell to the sand and lay on his side, not moving. He closed his eyes and fell asleep on the blessed sand outside of Abu Simbel. His dreams were happy and his soul was home.

"Come," said Michael. "Let him sleep and dream. He will be facing danger soon enough."

In the morning Thutmose woke to see the angels and Seth, with another god, throwing spears. "Ah. Thutmose, I presume. Morning, I'm Geb."

"Nice to meet you. I'm sure," said Thutmose. He had a feeling this god was not unfamiliar.

"Are you hungry?"

"No, I'm OK for now," said Thutmose.

"Great," said Seth. "Let's get started." As they walked away, Seth whispered to Thutmose, "Whatever you do, don't ask Geb how Nut is."

Thutmose whispered back, "I know what that means." Seth and Ariel laughed.

"A race," said Ariel. "You will race against Raguel. Whatever happens, I am sure there will be a good outcome." They all spread out and gave them space. "OK," said Ariel, "two miles, and no cheating!"

The sun was beginning to rise higher and the day was getting hot. The sand felt scorched under Thutmose's feet.

"RUN!" shouted Ariel, and they ran.

Raguel was running at what he considered to be a lazy pace as Thutmose struggled to keep up with him. Raguel turned around and ran backwards, beckoning Thutmose as he ran, and what was worse, Raguel was laughing. Thutmose was furious, but the angrier he got, it seemed the further Raguel was getting away from him. Raguel laughed out loud and folded his arms, still running backwards. Then he turned and with speed, disappeared. Suddenly the two miles were over. Raguel walked to Thutmose who was holding on to his knees. He put his hand on Thutmose's shoulder. "My brother, you are not human, stop acting like one," said Raguel. "You don't need to catch your breath; you could easily have outrun me. You should use your mind, not your body. Relax now, there will be another chance to beat me." He smiled and slapped Thutmose on the back. They jogged slowly back to the group waiting for them.

"Food," said Seth.

They all sat around but the only people eating were Seth,

Geb and Thutmose. "Why are we eating and they aren't?" Thutmose queried.

"Because it's what they do. We don't need to eat, but we thought you might feel out of place if we didn't."

"Don't eat on my behalf," said Thutmose. Thutmose, having been half human, still got hungry.

"Oh, it's fine," said Seth. "It's good to do something humany now and again."

"That's not even a word," said Thutmose.

"And that, my friend, is not really a sausage," laughed Geb.

After breakfast, they decided do an exercise on doppelgangers to get you out of sticky situations.

"Have you ever found yourself in a seriously sticky situation which you needed to get out of pretty pronto?" said Ariel. "Today, Thutmose, we are going to show you how it's done." He put his hand out to Michael. Michael stood up and in a short few seconds had an identical copy of himself standing next to him and he could converse with him and so could everyone else. Thutmose was amazed, and walked over to Michael's copy. It felt solid and it looked quizzically at him as he squeezed its arm, its shoulder. The doppelganger walked around Thutmose and touched his head, then as quickly as it had appeared, it disappeared.

Thutmose stepped back. "How did you do that?"

Michael walked over to Thutmose. "Close your eyes and imagine."

"Imagine what?"

"Imagine yourself. You are the very essence of yourself, no one else is. Bring out your essence. You have enough energy and knowledge combined inside you, to do this. It should be easy, easier than beating Raguel in a race."

Everyone laughed.

Thutmose closed his eyes, and imagined himself standing next to himself. He tried and tried, but it just wasn't happening.

Michael said, "OK, Thutmose, imagine a time when you felt happy and good about yourself. Were you dressed in your best finery? Had you achieved something amazing? Concentrate, it will come."

He stood still again and imagined himself, but suddenly there was a tug. He felt himself being pulled to the left. It tugged harder. He tried to open his eyes but couldn't. The angels and gods became concerned and stood around him.

Michael shouted, "Open your eyes, Thutmose. Open your eyes!" But suddenly he writhed and from out of his mouth came a red demon which slid next to him and stood up. It was Thutmose, but an ugly and evil Thutmose. The angels and the gods held hands in a circle; they absolutely could not allow it to escape.

"Thutmose!" shouted Metatron. "I command you to come back to us now. We want you back with us. Open your eyes."

Thutmose looked towards Metatron and his eyes looked pained. His doppelganger stood up. "You think this is going to help you? You couldn't be more wrong. Teach him all you like, but he will come to our side. When he does, we will take everything, and I mean everything." It clapped its hands and smiled, then it whipped its head around at speed. "Hi, Mikey. Be seeing ya, wouldn't wanna be ya." Then it was gone.

Thutmose fell to the floor. "Sorry, guys," he said. "It was a bit too powerful for me."

"It was your dad," said Michael.

"Lucifer can be a real shit sometimes," frowned Ariel.

Michael gave a half smile. "Let's call it a day, we can always try again tomorrow."

Thutmose walked back to the campsite outside of Abu Simbel and fell asleep. His dreams were disturbed. He was rolling and talking in tongues, he was sweating, then he was freezing. He dreamt of Hell, of fire, of beasts so ugly they made him cry out in his dreams. He screamed as though in agony; his cries rang out through the air. As dawn began to break, he became calmer.

"Luci is trying to weaken him," said Metatron. "We need to up our game and pretty fast."

When Thutmose awoke, he couldn't remember what he had dreamt, he just knew he hadn't slept very well.

It was Metatron's turn to show Thutmose how to protect himself. He spent the whole day with him showing how to grow a shield, how to use a blinding light, and how to throw a spear. Jophiel showed him how to shoot straight upwards at speed without motion sickness. It took Thutmose a few tries to get the hang of this one; he vomited more than once. Once he was feeling better, Metatron took Thutmose to one side. "Thutmose, how long have you been able to make yourself invisible?"

Thutmose thought. "I don't know, really, I only do it when I'm stressed or worried about getting caught, and to be honest in all the passing years, I've probably only been able to do it on purpose perhaps once, when I went to an office building when my father killed a man there."

"ONCE?" Thutmose looked shocked at Metatron's response. "Sorry, once, OK, once, it's fine, truly it is," said Metatron, "but you need to be able to do it spontaneously. Have you really no idea what you are capable of? You're a god. I know it was by accident, but haven't you tried anything over the time you have been alone?"

Thutmose looked embarrassed. "Well, I levitated…"

"Great, show me," said Metatron.

"I can't." Thutmose looked uncomfortable. "It was another accident. I was in bed at the time, erm, with someone, and we were sleeping and the next minute they left because they thought I was evil."

Metatron sighed. "Can you do anything on purpose?"

Thutmose had a sparkle in his eyes like that of a child opening a new toy at Christmas. "I can make fire…"

"Man has been able to do that since they were first put on the planet. Well, almost. You don't really mean with sticks, do you?" queried Metatron.

Thutmose closed his eyes and put his hands together. He had a look of deep concentration on his face, then as he widened his hands, he made a small flame, like a candle. He opened his eyes and looked at Metatron, who looked surprised, but then started laughing. Thutmose was furious. His eyes turned red and he knocked Metatron onto his back, who slid for 50 yards. Thutmose was breathing heavily and his shoulders were moving up and down. His face began to grimace and it looked like his body was beginning to swell. Metatron stood up and moved purposefully towards him. "Thutmose!" he yelled. "Stop it and stop it now." Thutmose began to slow his breathing. "Thutmose, I wasn't laughing at you, I was laughing with pleasure. Learn the difference. We can use your skill, we can make it, well, bigger!" Thutmose was returning to himself.

Metatron put his hand on Thutmose's shoulder and explained to him that if he let the anger take over, there would be nothing the angels and gods could do to keep him on side. He needed to be able to control his anger. They sat down on the sand and for the next two hours, Metatron taught Thutmose to vanish, at will. It was down to control and understanding the available energies around him, but understanding his own makeup. The angels had given him a gift and now, at this time in his existence, he was going to learn to use it. The more practice he gave it, Metatron told him, the quicker it would develop. He was able to access the very universe itself and remain there for as long as he wished, but he must always, without fail, be aware of who or what was there too.

Metatron had other things to teach him, but the moon was rising up in the heavens and the night was becoming chilly. They needed to get back to camp for support and protection and to make plans for the following day. Someone was watching in the darkness, and whilst Thutmose was too tired to notice, Metatron knew only too well who it was.

CHAPTER 16

Another day dawned and the training of Thutmose was heating up. Metatron approached Thutmose and beckoned him to meet someone new. Standing in front of him was a man whose strength was evident. He had short dark hair and was wearing an ancient Egyptian war outfit. He had a big beaming smile and held out a massive hand. "Good morning, brother." He smiled. "I'm truly pleased to meet you. I've heard a lot about you. Bruharis is the name and being the son of Seth is my game." He laughed loudly, throwing his head back. "I understand we have a lot in common and I'm here to show you some moves." With that, he flicked out his wings.

Thutmose wasn't quite sure what to say but smiled and shook his hand. "Seth, eh? Well, I agree, we certainly do have a lot in common."

"Great, let's get started," he said.

Bruharis started to dance around, hopping from foot to foot and making jokes. He kept flying punches out towards Thutmose and stopping within millimetres of actual impact. This man was fast. "How have you enjoyed the food whilst being here? Tasty, I hope, nutritious and fulfilling. A good meal creates a good body." Bruharis stood with his feet apart and his hands on his hips. He let Thutmose know that he had made the food and had always been a good cook. He had watched his mother from when he was a child, cooking all sorts of dishes, and he was blessed with a memory so sharp, he rarely forgot anything. Then he corrected himself and said that he never forgot anything. A big laugh followed. Thutmose definitely liked this fellow, there was a good aura about him.

Bruharis was born in the year 3500 in Jerusalem, in the time of King David. He was a popular child with the other children because he could give them rides on his back. They never discussed how different he was, they just loved him. They used to play at being soldiers and made up stories of brave soldiers who won battles and fair ladies. At the time, his wings were quite small. It was only when he grew older that the problems started. In his teenage years, Bruharis had started out as a blacksmith and was very good with horses. No matter how aggressive the horse, it became exceptionally calm in his presence. He knew he was destined for bigger things. As he got older, the wings inevitably grew bigger and strangely enough, it was a huge attraction for the women in the village. The men became very jealous of him, not just because of the attraction he seemed to emanate, but they also noticed he was not ageing. Rumours of witchcraft and devil worship surrounded him. One evening at the end of the summer season, the adult males in the village congregated together; they were going to cut off his wings and throw him from the village. His plan had been to fly away but before that happened, a great darkness had fallen upon the village and when it had dispersed, there were only women, children and teenagers remaining. They all feared him when he came out of his house and so he decided to leave anyway. The men of the village were never found; they had completely disappeared. He suspected that his father had been responsible, but it had never been proved.

Thutmose relayed his own story and they both found comfort in each other's misfortune. Neither would have chosen the father they had been destined to have. Thutmose wondered how long Bruharis had known about gods and angels. He told him ever since he was small. He knew things from a very early age and sadly knew when his parents, family and friends were going to die. He knew when and what ailment or accident would see their demise. He was not allowed to repeat it, though, or try to prevent it. It could change their fate and that could be detrimental to mankind and have all sorts of implications that would have resonated around the world, so unfortunately, he had to let the death take its course.

That had been the hardest part of growing up, losing all the people who meant so much to him. He didn't know that when he reached twenty-five, he would stop ageing. He used to check his appearance every day looking for signs of old age, but nothing ever happened – no wrinkles, no grey hair. Then the centuries moved on, and he went out of his way to find out what he was physically capable of; he was curious about his own abilities. He didn't have to do any strength work on his body, he reflected, it had developed on its own. He guessed that was a bonus of being a god. He could eat anything he liked and never put on weight. He got into fights and healed quickly, much faster than any normal human being. He enjoyed being immortal, but he had never had a long relationship with anyone. He didn't want to go through the pain of losing them, but that also meant he had not had children. He didn't know if the immortality would be passed on, and if it wasn't, then he would be in the position of watching his children grow up, and die of old age. He recollected some women had wanted to be with him purely for his 'curiosity', as he called it, it made him feel like a freak. But he had also learned over the years to hide his wings; he had the ability of being able to blend them into his body. No one would ever be able to tell that he was 'super different'. He had done quite well for himself and lived a life of luxury. He moved every few years so as not to give his secret away and occasionally, used materials to make himself look older and sometimes changed his hair colour. Funny thing about hair colour, it was like water, it didn't stick for long and literally dribbled off after a couple of days. He laughed so heartily at this, that the angels and gods laughed with him. Thutmose felt envious that during his time, Bruharis had achieved so much, and he had rather mourned his immortality rather than celebrated it and had absolutely no idea what his capabilities truly were. Bruharis said it was less risky these days, being who he was, as those who knew about him, who and what he was, were long dead.

As the sun started to set, Bruharis told Thutmose to stand. He was going to help him recognise when he was about to be physically assaulted. This required absolute concentration at the beginning, and he needed to tune in to the energy that was surrounding him. He told Thutmose to try to block a strike from his fist. Thutmose concentrated but Bruharis struck Thutmose on his cheek and he fell to the floor. Bruharis laughed. Thutmose was angry and quickly rose to his feet. His eyes flashed red. Bruharis put his hand up. "Thutmose, I know of your anger, but mine can match it. This is important. Deal with your anger and relax."

The angels stood watching and Metatron and Michael nodded to each other, but were ready to intervene if necessary.

Thutmose stood with his feet quite still. "Again," he said to Bruharis.

Bruharis struck Thutmose who stepped back, but did not fall. He became aware of the strength inside of his body and realised that he could remain standing.

"Again," he said.

Bruharis punched out at Thutmose who moved immediately. He had predicted the punch and had pushed his anger down into his stomach, having realised it was the anger which was making him unstable and confusing his energy. The angels and gods looked at each other and realised they were making headway. Everyone felt the confidence growing in Thutmose and it appeared that he was beginning to realise that he was more than human, he was a god.

"Again, harder," Thutmose demanded.

Bruharis tried to hit him so hard, the ground on which he was standing shook, but at the last second, Thutmose caught his hand and smiled, then he disappeared. Bruharis, caught unaware, was suddenly plunged to the floor. His sandal laces were quickly tied together and he was suddenly chucked up into the air and was bent over and moving at quite a speed away from the group, then suddenly he was spun around and brought straight back to the group, and stood up straight, but he fell over, having lost his orientation from the dizzying spin he had received a few seconds earlier and the fact his laces were tied. Thutmose reappeared and suddenly everyone started to laugh. "Well done, well done, Thutmose," they cheered. Bruharis was laughing so much, he couldn't get back up again. Thutmose, ever the gentleman helped him up and they shook hands.

Calling it a day, they made their way back to the camp site

outside Abu Simbel. They agreed that the next day, they would once again attempt for Thutmose to create his doppelganger. Thutmose was nervous but felt he could achieve this. They all sat down in a large circle and decided that this evening, they would relax and celebrate. The angels and gods were looking forward to a drink, except Metatron and Michael who were keeping watch. Metatron had told Michael about the watcher in the darkness. They walked away from Abu Simbel into the night and waited.

As the moon began to rise, they saw a figure approaching them; it was hunched and appeared to be dragging its legs. They smelled it before they saw it fully. "Evening, gentlemen!" it shouted.

Metatron and Michael looked at each other. "Azazel?" they said in unison.

Azazel stretched up his arms and straightened up. Due to his incarceration by God, Azazel appeared as a spectre. "Well, you haven't forgotten me then?"

"No, why would we?" Michael said.

"Well, you know… anyway, I see you have Thutmose. His father isn't too happy about it, but he has an agreement with our dad and he can't go anywhere near him, so I'm it. Any chance I can meet Thutmose?"

"No, you can't," said Metatron.

"Well, no harm in asking." Azazel smiled. "I guess we will be meeting him soon enough."

Azazel's spectre turned into an angel, but his overall look was grey and dull. His hair was lank and eyes sunken, but his physique was still strong. When the moon shone down, he almost disappeared. "This is what I hate about coming up here," said Azazel. "Bloody moon." Metatron and Michael laughed. Azazel frowned, but then he laughed too. Just for a moment, a little flash of light cascaded through his wings. He looked at Metatron and Michael. "I have a message for you, and it is this." He paused. "We are coming in our thousands. You won't have the army. It won't last long, and we will take him. You can train him all you like, but you won't succeed. He is his father's son, and you cannot change his loyalty. If you let him come now, he will have the best of both worlds. One half of the year up here, one half of the year down there." A bony finger pointed towards the ground. "Well?"

"You know the answer, Azazel. His name is Thutmose, not Persephone, and even though he is Lucifer's son, you forget his mother was human. I can pretty much guarantee, we have a bigger army on our side than you could possibly fathom."

"Don't be ridiculous," said Azazel. "We come from the same family; I know everything you know."

"We know," smiled Metatron, "but we have to show some sort of bluff."

"I guess so," grinned Azazel. "Does he know what will happen?"

"He knows we will be battling for him and he will be well prepared," said Michael.

Azazel nodded slightly. "I've never had peace, you know, but that was my curse. I was blamed for making man stray and for teaching him about war."

Michael looked at Azazel with sympathy. "You were wrong, Azazel, your teachings have brought the world into disrepute. The battles now are wrought with more fury and violence than should ever have been allowed."

Azazel smirked. "When the student is ready, the teacher

appears, Michael."

"The wrong teacher appeared," Michael said.

Azazel stared at both Michael and Metatron, then he turned. "You *will* lose and you are foolish to attempt to keep him from us. Well, I had best be off. Fried priest tonight." He licked his fingers.

"You truly are disgusting," said Michael.

Azazel laughed and walked back into the darkness. He changed as he made his way back and would slide back into his body on reaching the underground.

"We're safe to go now," said Metatron. They turned and started back towards the camp. They could hear the party in full swing.

"It would have been useful to have Azazel on our side," said Michael.

Metatron said nothing. They knew that if there was any chance of them losing, God would destroy the earth he loved so much.

CHAPTER 17

Everyone woke with a buzz. Having had an enjoyable evening and laughed a lot, everyone was feeling more relaxed. Bruharis had a made a very hearty breakfast which everyone enjoyed. He had flown secretly, into Cairo, to pick up fresh ingredients. Once everyone was ready it was time for Thutmose to try to produce his doppelganger again. Everyone stood around and waited, and waited, and waited and waited.

"Thutmose?" said Michael. "Thutmose?" There was a burst of laughter; he had fallen asleep on his feet.

Metatron put his hand on his shoulder. Thutmose opened his eyes with a start. "You fell asleep. We were… Are you alright?"

Thutmose, nodded. "Yes, I'm fine. I was in a space, dark space. I haven't seen it before, but I knew which way to go. I could see even though it was dark. I felt like there were people there but I don't know who. There was a vibration through my body."

"Hmmm, shouldn't worry about it too much," said Raphael. "Anyone who was there was probably coming to have a good look at you. If you have crossed boundaries, they will want to know how and why you did it. Did anyone speak to you or touch you?"

"No… but I thought… The feeling is different than before."

"Ah, well, just make sure if it happens again, you don't walk too far. Sometimes you can go too far and then not find your way back. Funny, that, you can go forwards, but you can't go backwards." Raphael gave a half smile.

"You can give this test a miss; it might be safer," said Michael.

"I'd rather get it over with, to be honest, you'll never know when I might need it. Best to make sure I can do it, right?" Thutmose gave a slight nod.

"That's the spirit," said Metatron.

Thutmose closed his eyes. After a slight pause, his doppelganger appeared. He opened his eyes and looked at it. "Is that truly me?"

"Well, yes and no," said Raphael. "Obviously it knows everything you know, talks like you, walks like you, but it's dispensable. Once it's gone, its gone, literally. Good job, though."

Everyone agreed. Bes walked forward; he had just arrived. An ugly but popular Egyptian god, he was a good protector from evil. "They're a good distraction," said Bes. "If you are running one way, send the doppelganger the opposite way, even if it's off a cliff. They don't feel pain and when its time is up, it usually disperses at the last second. Good confusion tactic for the enemy."

Thutmose looked at himself. "Hello," he said.

"Hello back," said the doppelganger. Thutmose closed his eyes and concentrated. When he opened them, the doppelganger was gone.

"Well done," said Michael.

As the morning progressed, they showed Thutmose new and frightening fighting skills. He was fast but not faster than the angels. "We need to show him an alternative to be able to move away from Lucifer." Michael was clearly worried. "Lucifer is the fastest angel I have ever seen, besides myself, and sometimes, even I can't move fast enough especially if he changes. He knows my skills, we have fought often enough, but he can be remarkable. Something has to surprise him, something he doesn't expect."

"I think we have the answer." They turned. "Sobek and Serqet," laughed Bes. "Good to see you, my friends, how have you been?"

"Wet and dry for a very long time." They laughed.

Raphael looked at them quizzically. "So what are you doing here?"

"Wherever there is a battle in the sands, the scorpion always looks for prey." Serqet winked.

"And wherever there is a battle by water, I get fed well," laughed Sobek, rubbing his stomach. "Thutmose is a god, we hear, so he can use us to escape his enemy. Enemy gets too close on the sand, he gets stung. Enemy gets too close by the water, he gets eaten."

Michael flinched. "Well, you are all welcome here. Please join in the company."

As they walked along, Serqet said, "I understand he belongs to a god of the underworld. Is that correct?"

"Yes," said Metatron, "and here he is. Thutmose, may I introduce Serqet and Sobek, not that you won't recognise them already."

"Oh my," said Serqet. "You are handsome." The scorpion on her head wiggled approvingly. Thutmose stepped back. "Oh, don't worry about him," smiled Serqet. "I can put him away any time."

Sobek grabbed her by the arm, "So sorry, she's been in the sun too long," and he pulled her away.

Thutmose looked after them. "I hope she's focussed in battle."

"You have no idea," said Metatron.

News of the forthcoming battle was getting out and more gods were joining the army. Whilst they were talking tactics, there was a whirl of dust which seemed to throw itself over the rocks. Leaping from rock to rock, the cloud got closer and closer. Then suddenly, *thud*, right next to Thutmose. The tallest and widest baboon stood up and looked at everyone like he wanted to fight. "So, when does it start?"

Bes, looked up and up. "Babi, how did you find out?"

"Nothing gets past me," he growled. "Want to make something of it?"

"Nope, not at all." Bes stepped back. "Your reputation precedes you." He bowed.

"You are welcome here, Babi," smiled Raphael.

Babi grunted. "Anyone to eat round here?" he said.

"There will be," said Metatron, "but best to see Bruharis over there, he's in charge of food."

Babi looked down at Thutmose and said nothing. "Are you sure?" He looked at Raphael and nodded in Thutmose's direction.

"Good grief, no," said Raphael.

"He's the one we're battling for," frowned Michael.

"But I can…"

"Yes, we know," said Michael, "but it's his father's fault, not his."

Babi gave one last sniff above Thutmose's head. "Hmm," he said, then wandered off towards Bruharis.

"What the… Why does everyone keep sniffing me?" said Thutmose.

"It's your smell," said Metatron.

"My what??" Thutmose shrieked.

"Your smell, but don't worry, not everyone can smell it."

"SMELL WHAT?" said Thutmose.

"The rotting corpse smell. Anyway, let's—"

"WHOA, WHOA, WHOA," said Thutmose.

"You riding a horse?" Metatron said sarcastically.

"What the… smell… corpse… why didn't I know that?"

Metatron rolled his eyes. "Because… Thutmose… you have never bothered to get in touch with yourself. You have carried on century after century, wondering why some people knew who you were, and some didn't."

"What, why…? So can everyone smell me?" he said.

Metatron looked at him with a blank face. "You really didn't hear a word I just said, did you?" Metatron sighed heavily. "Not everyone can smell you, just those of us who are a little different."

"Little different?" shrieked Thutmose. "We're bloody more than a little different, or didn't you notice that some oversized talking monkey just stood next to me?"

In one second – *WHACK!* – he was up against a rock and flat on the sand.

"Don't EVER call me a monkey again," said Babi and stormed back towards the food.

"Are you alright?" said Michael.

"And stop asking me if I'm bloody alright," said Thutmose, standing up and dusting himself off. "Of course I'm not alright. One minute I'm living a fairly liveable life in Paris with clothes, and money, and cupboards and a bed and clothes and… and the next I'm in Abu Simbel, with a load of strange people I don't know, who are telling me my dad is going to take me to Hell. I'm getting possessed, de-possessed, thrown on the floor, beaten in races, thrashed by a mo— baboon. So no, no, I AM NOT OK." He was screaming, stamping his feet and swinging his arms, then he threw himself on the sand. Everyone stopped what they were doing and just stared at him, shocked at his outburst. This was truly unexpected. Thutmose was breathing heavily and began coughing up sand into his mouth, and then began choking.

"Oh, hell, not this again," said Jophiel. They ran towards him and stood him up.

"Leave me alone. Just go away," said Thutmose. They let him go and he stormed off towards the rocks.

"Too bloody human if you ask me," said Babi.

"Well no one asked you, Babi," said Metatron. Babi growled.

As Thutmose sat on a high rock, he noticed a vulture swirling overhead. He felt a draught and a woman was standing next to him. "Hello," she said.

Thutmose looked up. "Oh, great, who the hell are you?" he said.

"Well that's a fine hello," she said. "You're Egyptian, you should know who I am. I was just flying over your head. I know who you are." She smiled. Thutmose said nothing. "Why so sad?" she said. Thutmose still said nothing, then looked at her again and the kindness in her face broke down his barrier. He explained to her briefly, the most recent happenings. Nekhbet smiled. "Well, you could always end it, you know, but you need to do it the right way. Your father has to tell you, though, it's a generation thing. We aren't allowed to tell you how to finish it all."

Thutmose looked at her. "I know, the angels told me as much. I don't know if I want to meet my father. I think he wants to hurt me."

Nekhbet looked out across the horizon. She had met Lucifer in the past and he had injured her too. "It's his nature," she said. "He never used to be like that. When he was first born, he was remarkable. God took such care…" Her voice drifted off. "Anyway, you always have a choice, and don't worry too much about the smell thing." She smiled. "Some of the other gods stink too… Just get up close and personal and you'll know what I mean." She stood up and stretched out her arms. "I'm on your side, you know. I have to fly until I see them coming, then I'll come and let you know. I can usually give people plenty of time to prepare, but Lucifer's army moves fast, very fast. They are like dust. I'll be seeing you." She smiled and shot up into the sky.

Thutmose wondered how she knew that Lucifer's army moved fast. Where had she seen it before? Maybe he was looking too much into it. He slid off the rock and made his way back to the group. Feeling a bit sheepish about his tantrum, he sauntered up to Bruharis.

Bruharis slapped him on the back. "So, Thutmose my friend. What do you want to eat?" Thutmose smiled and picked at the meat and naan breads he chose. He sat down. Metatron sat with him.

"I'm sorry for my harshness," said Metatron. "I think I'm just a bit nervous, as you no doubt are."

Thutmose stopped eating. He looked at Metatron. "It's going to be bad, isn't it?" Thutmose looked down at his food, not really feeling hungry.

Metatron thought about his answer; he could lie, but Thutmose deserved more than that. "Yes, yes, it is," he said, "but we will fight to the end for you. All of us here will be by your side as much as possible during the battle. If you get so frightened that you can't cope, come and find me. No matter what I am doing, I will look after you. So will Michael, Jophiel, Raphael, Bes… all of us, Thutmose. The last thing we want is for your father to take you and we have the biggest weapon of all." Thutmose looked at Metatron, who pointed up towards the sky. "Our father…" Thutmose smiled.

Michael was glad that Thutmose was distracted. He knew he was to have a final discussion with God. He walked away from the group, up to the Temple of Abu Simbel, looked up towards the sky, stretched his wings and flew. God was waiting for him when he arrived. "Michael, I understand we have a lot to talk about. Walk with me," said God.

CHAPTER 18

God looked at Michael and smiled. He told him he had been watching and that he had done a good job with Thutmose. Thutmose was a fast learner, like his father. Both God and Michael agreed that it was now up to Thutmose to perfect his fighting technique. Michael would return to Abu Simbel and he would return Thutmose back to his home in Paris. It would give Thutmose the opportunity to put his house in order should he not return. God had one last comment to make to Michael which was that if Thutmose were to be possessed by Lucifer in battle, God would not hesitate to destroy him. He would not allow a son of Lucifer to stay on the earth and take on the same attributes as his father.

Michael told God he remembered, too, that Thutmose had murdered the accountant without any guilt and had been prepared to dispose of the body, so was untrustworthy, he realised that. But God just smiled and said, "Not everything is as it seems, Michael."

When Michael returned to Abu Simbel the party had quietened down and Thutmose was asleep. Thutmose had purposely got drunk. "Well," noted Metatron, "at least he won't have a hangover in the morning. That's one good thing about being a god."

Michael, the angels and the Egyptian gods talked about the issues that he had discussed with God. Michael stressed it was absolutely vital that everyone kept a very close eye on Thutmose, even during the heat of battle, to ensure that he was behaving as a god of his stature should. If anyone noticed anything unusual in his behaviour, like he was attacking people on their side, then they were to report to Michael straight away. Michael reiterated to them God's final decision.

In the morning the sun rose high and the heat of the day became intense very quickly. During the evening the camp had been dismantled and no one would have been able to tell that anyone had ever been there. Michael approached Thutmose and told him it was time to leave for Paris. What he was going to show Thutmose now was the last thing that would be of help to him in any dire moment. He put his hands onto Thutmose's shoulders and told him to think of being at home in Paris. He told him to concentrate as hard as he could on his house, and wish to be home; he didn't even have to close his eyes. Thutmose saw the beauty of Paris through the centuries. He thought of the times he had visited Paris, he thought of his home, and within seconds, there he was. It was so quiet. He looked around his house and he could hardly believe that he was at home having been in Abu Simbel no less than two minutes earlier. This gift he had encountered, the years he had wasted not knowing what he was capable of, seemed incredible now. He walked into his library and went to his cupboard safe. He removed from the top drawer a large key. He walked over to his extensive bookcase and put the key into a lock behind a very ancient book. He pulled a door open and walking down a long corridor, there was a very large wooden door at the end with a concealed room behind it.

In the room was a huge desk which was very intricately

carved, with matching drawers situated all around the room. The room had a thick velvet carpet running through it, such luxury usually only found in palaces of kings and queens. Thutmose had been given the carpet by Charles the 1st as he had not liked the deep red colour. Charles told him it reminded him of pools of blood; almost predictive, Thutmose reflected. He walked around to his seat at the desk and pulled open the drawers. He removed documents from the drawer and signed each one at the bottom. The items he had collected over the centuries would be donated to charities. Each envelope he had put the documents into had the name of the charity carefully written across the front.

Thutmose poured himself a glass of whiskey, and spent the next hour or so wandering around his house appreciating all that he had obtained through his very long lifetime. He wandered out to the veranda and stared across Paris and remembered it in its infancy. He also remembered the time of King Louis and Marie Antoinette. He had been present when the peasants of Paris had removed King Louis and Marie Antoinette's heads. It was a dreadful sight to see, but the citizens of Paris partied for many days and inevitably, Paris was changed forever. After that incident, he left Paris and did not return for over 100 years. He made his way to Britain, despite the fact Britain was at war with France. On the 18th of June 1815, he was to be a witness as Napoleon was beaten at Waterloo. He thought about Bruharis and the envy he had felt towards him, but on contemplation, perhaps his long life had not been so wasted after all. In every battle he had been witness to, he had in fact given comfort to the disabled and dying. Night was drawing in and he made his way to his very elegant bedroom.

Just as he was about to get into bed he heard a voice say, "Sleep well, because it may be the last sleep you ever get." Thutmose was not afraid; there had been too many weird incidents happening over the last few days.

He climbed into bed and fell into a deep, peaceful sleep. He dreamt of Abu Simbel, his past in Cairo. He could see people so clearly it was almost as if he were truly there. He dreamt of the completion of the pyramids as they stood out in all their gleaming white glory in the sunshine of Cairo. He was transported to the Sphinx, which seemed so real that when he reached out to touch it, he could feel the sand under his fingers. He felt a tap on his shoulder and when he turned around, he saw it was Bruharis. "Are you in my dream, am I dreaming of you?"

Bruharis smiled. "No," he said, "we are both really here, it's just your body is back in Paris, and your soul has come to where it truly wants to be. I spend a lot of time here too, but mostly I spend it in Alexandria and I always choose to be there before the great fire destroyed the library."

Thutmose looked quizzically at Bruharis. "So we can literally decide where we want to be, what time we want to be there? We can walk around as though we are truly there, but we can't interact with people? Wow, we really are a weird bunch, aren't we?"

"I guess you could say that it is verging on the point of voyeurism," laughed Bruharis. "We can even go and watch ourselves from any particular point in time, but I tend not to do this because I am regularly surrounded my friends and family and I find it quite an upsetting experience. It brings back memories which can stay with you for days and it really puts you off your stride."

Thutmose and Bruharis walked around Cairo. They chatted idly and when they had walked for what appeared to have been all night, Bruharis shook hands with Thutmose and said, "Ding, ding. Time to wake up."

Thutmose opened his eyes and sat on the end of his bed for a few moments. It was an extraordinary experience, or a truly weird interactive type of dream. He felt happier even though he knew what was coming. He walked into his kitchen and made himself a coffee, and walked out onto his veranda and took one last look across Paris. The sun was high and as autumn was drawing near, it was a truly beautiful day. He felt the battle was near, and was even more sure about it when he walked back into his living room and saw the spectre of Azazel. Azazel did not need to introduce himself. "I know you." Azazel looked grey but Thutmose could see him clearly. "Why are you here, Azazel? You will be seeing me soon enough. Who sent you here? My father?"

Azazel stepped forward but as the sun was shining in through the window he partly disappeared. "You see, I really don't need to answer that question because you already know the answer. I could not have come here of my own volition, your father would not have been happy. I come with an offer. Your father could not come himself because he is a son of God. God, in his infinite and knowledgeable wisdom, has told your father not to come anywhere near you because if he did, he would destroy him and his kingdom. Your true father loves you and wants you to be with him eternally. You could help him bring to justice those on the earth who insist on doing wrong. If you do so he will ensure that when the end of the world finally happens, whilst he will be in purgatory, you will have your place at the right hand of God. Whilst he may be the lost sheep of God's family, there would be no need for you to suffer the same consequences. So, what is your answer?"

Thutmose smiled. "Goodbye, Azazel. I would shake your hand but instead I bow to you. Let it never be said that I, as an ancient Egyptian, forgot my manners in the presence of such a grand and elegant emissary."

Azazel stepped back into the shadow to make himself more visible. "You are making a huge mistake, Thutmose. At least walk with me and let me know your reasoning?"

Thutmose thought for a minute. He was sure he had time. "We can walk through dimensions, so please, what is your pleasure?"

Thutmose thought about the mountains of Sweden, the Himalayas, but settled for the streets of Paris instead. Azazel smiled and they set out. "It's going to look like you are talking to yourself," he laughed.

"Doesn't matter, people think I'm crazy most of the time anyway."

They walked and Azazel talked idly about how he came to Earth, what skills he brought to mankind and the trouble he was in when God knew what the Watchers had done. Thutmose listened and almost felt sorry for Azazel, but told him it was his own fault for giving in to his baser instincts. Azazel kept talking and Thutmose had not taken much notice about where they walking to. He suddenly looked up. "Oh, Azazel, what have you done?" Thutmose had been so busy counting the cracks on pavements in the streets of Paris, he failed to notice when Azazel flicked the dimensional curtain aside and had walked Thutmose straight into Hell.

Thutmose turned to look at Azazel, who on home ground,

had become solid and his angelic size towered over Thutmose. Known for creating war, Azazel was dressed in armour that looked like it had been created by a battalion of soldiers. It was solid and golden, his huge wings stretched out and rather than looking angelic, he looked fierce. "Welcome home, Thutmose, your father is waiting."

Fire and lava spat around Thutmose, ice on black burned trees appeared and melted, screams surrounded him and he closed off his ears. He felt a vibration in the ground. Looking up, he saw the brightest of lights approaching him at speed. It was Lucifer. Even from a distance, his rage was palpable. Thutmose had to think fast. "I'll leave you to it," said Azazel, and he was gone.

Thutmose could do nothing but watch as his father ploughed towards him. Lucifer stopped before reaching Thutmose. He could smell the fear running through his son and felt conflicting emotions. Lucifer had flashes of when Thutmose had been created, the moment he had impregnated his mother. Thutmose was real. He saw him again on the night he was born, he saw him as he was growing up and the life he had been resolved to endure. But as easily as the emotions had risen, Lucifer put them away with a flick of his fingers. His soul was empty of any feeling towards Thutmose and besides, he had refused the chance that Azazel had offered him, so why should he care how his son thought or felt? He walked towards Thutmose, and Lucifer in all his beautiful and bountiful glory, stood over him. He wanted that energy and it would stop a war if he just took it now.

"Well, didn't think I would see you here." He folded his arms. "You turned down my offer and why exactly? Let me think." Lucifer drew a long-clawed finger across his mouth.

"You have been wanting to speak to me. Well, here I am… Ask."

Thutmose tried to speak, but his throat had dried up.

"Nothing to say, eh? Well, let me see if I can help you out. You are bored of your immortal life and you want out?"

Still, Thutmose could not speak.

"You have had a long and tedious life and you want to go to Heaven? Heaven, Heaven, Heaven." Lucifer's voice was getting louder with each mention; his fingers were jabbing upwards with each word. "Why? Why do you want this? I am your father. You could have the world if you would only love me and be with me, by my side, as my heir."

Thutmose began to recite a prayer inside his head, and Lucifer turned and looked with such hatred, Thutmose thought he would die at any moment. Lucifer began to change. "I met you as an angel because I thought it would help you transition," Lucifer said. "I did this all for you." He was changing slowly into a repulsive demon. "You don't seem to have grasped the practicalities of your situation. Let me explain. Whether you like it or not, I am your father. I was born at the beginning of time, and I can change the moon, the stars, the sea, the winds, the rain. Because you are my son, I own you, I own your soul, I own your life. You belong completely to me. If you refuse me now, your fate will be much worse than you could imagine. When the battle is won and we have you, you will wish that you had not treated me with so little respect. I will win the battle and the war and the world will weep at the sight of the destruction that I will have wrought. Your decision is careless and ill thought out. You are stupid, Thutmose; do you think that they will want you once the battle is over? They will not look for you, they don't even care for you, really. They are using you. When push comes to shove, they will send you down. Do you honestly think anyone is looking for you now? They have sent you home, Thutmose, because you are a liability. Did you forget about the murder you committed? Did you forget that I disposed of the mess for you?"

Thutmose had not been asleep when Michael had returned from his meeting with God. He knew that if he were to change sides willingly or otherwise, he would be destroyed. He reflected on the number of years he had lived and knew that he had often wished for his own demise, however, destruction like this had never been on his list of choices; he would rather die in battle. Thutmose knew his choice was being taken from him. He looked to the heavens and softly whispered, "Father, I don't know if you can hear me, if you can, or even if you want to because of who I am, but please, Father, give me the courage that I need to fight. Please give me the confidence to fight with my brothers and the ability to support them as they support me, and if I am to die in Hell please don't let me go like this. Please don't make me live in Hell, please let me come home."

God was listening and heard every word that Thutmose said. He felt Thutmose's heart and knew it was true, but he was still Lucifer's son. God sat back and thought about the options that he could give Thutmose, but he held firm. If Thutmose's soul was compromised in battle and he could not resist, there would be no other option than to finish him. The energy Thutmose now held within, could be as destructive as a nuclear bomb.

Lucifer was furious; his anger became completely out of control. "How dare you? How dare you call to him? This is my kingdom, MY KINGDOM! You belong to me, whether you like it or not. You are MINE! How dare you not love me? ME, the first born, the highest of all archangels, the beautifulness of God himself! How dare you? How dare you?" Lucifer raged and stamped; his minions were running for cover. He smashed and destroyed rocks and flew around spitting fire, then suddenly he stopped, towering over Thutmose, all became quite still. "Our Father will destroy me and I am going to destroy you… right… now…"

Michael was waiting in Thutmose's home. He heard God and knew instantly where Thutmose was, but as soon as Michael knew, the other angels knew too.

"Bloody hell," said Jophiel. "Not this again. This situation with Thutmose is beginning to feel like Groundhog Day. If we go and fetch him, we'll miss the battle and all will be lost."

Michael smiled and in a split second, Thutmose was back in his living room. "It's time, Thutmose."

Thutmose saw the most beautiful angel he had ever seen. Michael was standing in the brightest light and his armour and wings were at their most stunning. The colours of the rainbow and colours outside of the spectrum ran up and down his wings and Thutmose could have sworn Michael's wings were two or three times the size that he had ever seen.

"Bloody hell, Michael, you look fantastic," said Thutmose.

"Thanks," he smiled, "I have that impact on a lot of people. You aren't looking too bad yourself. Bad afternoon?"

Thutmose began to laugh. "And not a second too soon." He smiled.

"Shit," said Lucifer. "I bloody hate it when that happens."

CHAPTER 19

"Good armour. Roman, then?"

"Yes," said Thutmose. "I was going to go for my Thermopylae armour, but I couldn't find the helmet and I didn't want to mix the two, I'd feel really stupid."

"So is it heavy?" Michael asked.

"No, not really," said Thutmose. "I'm a god, so it feels quite light, really."

"Good," said Michael. "We need to know you can move quickly."

"Well if it gets too heavy, I'll drop a bit off."

"Well don't get too exposed," said Michael. "Not that it will matter in this battle. If a bit drops off, its usually cut off by someone or something. Anyway, best get moving."

"Shall I concentrate?" said Thutmose. Michael put his hand on Thutmose's shoulder and before Thutmose could pronounce his name, they were in Egypt. "Bugger," said Thutmose. "That was fast."

"Well at least you didn't vomit," said Jophiel.

Thutmose looked around and there was a throng of angels. As far as the eye could see, there were white wings and Egyptian gods and just when Thutmose thought it couldn't get any better a voice hollered out, "Thutmose, Thutty, oy, Thutmose!" He recognised the voice and there was Tutankhamen. "It's all real, man," he said. "All that I went through when I died, it's real. I'm here… Whoo-hoo. Look, look, I've brought a chariot and guess what? Knives on the wheels, dude! This is so cool and guess what? Guess what? If I die, right, it's OK because I can get back on and go again, it's like a circus, dude."

"It's great to see you!" shouted Thutmose.

"Dude!" Tutankhamen shouted back. "Who would have thought it? You, a devil egg? Here's me fighting for you. Oh, this is so, so cool. Can we have a drink after?"

Thutmose looked at Michael. There was a sadness in Thutmose's eyes. Michael turned. "Yes, Tutty, of course he can."

Tutankhamen laughed. "Great. Tutty and Thutty out on the town."

Thutmose smiled and looked to the front. He saw Bruharis who put his hand up. Thutmose put his hand up. "Great guy."

"Yes, yes he is," said Michael.

Thutmose looked at Michael. "He's coming."

"I know."

A sandstorm started, the sky began to grow dark, the angels grew brighter to give enough light. It began to rain and the rain mixed with the sand, making it sludgy. Metatron looked at Michael. "He's doing this to make it difficult to walk."

Michael said nothing, then it began to snow.

"It's a tactic," said Thutmose. "He'll freeze us next so your wings will be heavy with sand and ice."

"You know his strategy?" queried Metatron.

"Yes, yes I do," said Thutmose. "After all, he's my dad. Do you think God could bring out the sun?"

"Ask him," said Michael.

Thutmose looked at Michael. "Do you think he will hear me?"

Michael winked. Thutmose looked up at the sky and suddenly everyone put their heads down. "Go on," said Michael and nudged Thutmose.

"Father, it's Thutmose here," he said. Michael and Metatron looked at each other and smiled. "My dad has made it wet and sandy and snowy. Is there any chance you could send the sun to melt it all, please, and dry the sand?" The sun suddenly shone brightly, hot and high and a big cheer went up.

He heard Tutankhamen. "Dude, cool."

"I really will kill him," fumed Lucifer.

"Well done, Thutmose," said Metatron.

Bes walked over to Thutmose. "So, Thutmose, you know his strategy? What is it?"

"I can't tell you," Thutmose replied.

"Hmm, can't or won't."

"Won't," said Thutmose. "That would be cheating."

Bes looked perplexed. "Thutmose, Lucifer IS a cheat. We could save ourselves from this battle, if you told us what his strategy was. We could cut him off at the pass, as it were."

Thutmose said nothing. Bes looked furious.

"Bes," Metatron said, "if you don't want to fight, then you are free to leave."

"That's not the point, is it?" said Bes. "Thutmose knows his strategy, but chooses not to say anything," he said sarcastically. "Have you any idea how many of us could get hurt in this battle?"

"I think I can stop most of that," said a female voice, and from a few rows behind came Iside.

"You look wonderful, Iside," smiled Michael.

"Thank you," she said. "I feel it. I have a debt to pay and not just to Geb. Hello, Thutmose, you look gorgeous." Thutmose blushed.

Bes threw his hands up. "Great, let's all have a mutual appreciation party on the front line, whilst Lucifer marches towards us with a whole army of bloody psychopaths. Why don't we just ask him if he wants something to eat?"

"Oh, you don't need to ask Lucifer if he wants something to eat," said Raphael, in a matter-of-fact voice. "He eats anyone and anything anyway." Laughter rang out across the lines.

Bes walked away and joined his line again. "Just don't come to me if he chews your bloody leg off," he said.

"It won't be just your leg he eats," said Jophiel.

"Piss off, Jophiel," snapped Bes.

Suddenly the ground started to vibrate and as they looked ahead, they could see Lucifer. The vibration became more violent, so much so that the ground was moving.

"There must be a few of them," said Raphael. "Unless he's brought his skateboard and it's had new batteries." A titter rippled through the lines, but then the vibration stopped.

An exceptionally bright blinding light shone, and then a voice boomed out. "Thutmose!"

"Do not move," said Michael. Thutmose looked at Michael. All the angels were now their heavenly size and dwarfed Thutmose, Bruharis and the other gods. Michael looked down at Thutmose. "Do not move."

The voice boomed out again. "Thutmose."

"Do not move," said Michael. "He knows he cannot come for you. God told him to stay away. He's been let off once today. If he makes you go to him then the die is cast."

"I can stop the battle," said Thutmose.

"But you will create Hell on Earth," said Metatron. "It's not just your soul we are fighting for, it's the whole of mankind."

"Thutmose!" the voice boomed out again.

Michael stepped forward. "I'll go to him." Thutmose put his hand on a feather on Michael's wing. Michael looked down at him and smiled. "I'll be fine, we're old friends." Michael looked up and frowned. He knew Lucifer's temper and Michael felt today, Lucifer was particularly dangerous.

Walking towards him, Michael drew in his wings; this was a gesture of friendliness. He took his hand away from his sword and approached Lucifer. Lucifer was seething, not least because he could not get Thutmose to come to him. "Lucifer." Michael put his hand out to him. Lucifer was looking past him.

"Thutmose!" Lucifer boomed out.

"Lucifer," said Michael, "he will not come to you. Please, look at me. Lucifer, look at me."

Lucifer could hardly stop glancing past Michael. "Thutmose!" Lucifer screamed. His eyes were flashing red, then reptilian, then mother of pearl. His frustration was plain. Parts of Lucifer were switching from angel, to demon, to reptilian.

"Lucifer, my brother, please." Michael put his hand on Lucifer's arm. Lucifer looked at Michael's hand, and then his eyes, and then the fast breathing began to slow down. "He will not come to you, Lucifer; he is our responsibility today."

Lucifer began to calm down and returned to his angelic self. His colours ran and trickled and he shone brightly. "Well, Mikey, have you missed me?"

"Always," said Michael. When they looked at each other the kindness and compassion that moved through Michael's eyes made Lucifer still.

Thutmose whispered to Metatron, "Does my dad always look like that? I mean, he's amazing, isn't he?"

Metatron laughed. Jophiel looked sideways at Metatron. "It's only Michael who can make Lucifer look like that, trust me," said Jophiel. "We were robbed." The angels laughed, but it was true. The bond between Michael and Lucifer would always be strong, despite the fact that Michael threw Lucifer out of Heaven. It was very much a love-hate relationship.

Lucifer looked at Michael. "I miss you; I miss you and I hate it, it hurts me, and you don't care, you don't care, you hurt me and you don't care. I miss you."

"I know," said Michael. "I feel it every time I see you, but you hate me too."

"Only because you're ugly," said Lucifer. They both gave a little laugh.

"Why are we fighting, Lucifer?" Michael asked.

"You know why, Mikey. I haven't got long."

"But wouldn't you rather do your time and then speak to Father to see what he can do?"

"No," said Lucifer. "I just want more time. Our father won't give me more time, he's going to throw me into everlasting fire."

Michael looked at him. "And do you think acting this way is the best approach?"

Lucifer's eyes flashed red. "And how else do you think things should be handled, Michael? Thutmose is my son and he would be able to help me last longer if he wasn't such a selfish child. He doesn't care about me, he doesn't care how many dead bodies I have to get or how many souls I have to burn, crush, divide – he's a selfish child, he's selfish." Lucifer's mouth was grimacing and his voice was becoming tight and high pitched.

"He isn't selfish, Lucifer. In years he's a child compared to us; he's hardly lived. We have been here since the beginning of time. What he found was accidental, it was my fault. I should have moved it years before they started to create the pyramids. Thutmose needed a hand to help him through the years, and…"

Lucifer tilted his head down and looked up with red eyes at Michael, interrupting his speech. "Who do you think has helped him during the years, Michael? It was me. Our father who art in bloody Heaven said I couldn't go near him but I could help him if necessary, so I have. All I want now is payback. He owes me. He owes me." Lucifer began to get angry and was stamping his feet and clenching his fists. "I want more time, Mikey, more time, and he can give it to me."

Michael put his hand on Lucifer's arm. "You don't have that option, Lucifer. You are not as almighty as our father is." Lucifer began to pant.

Ariel looked at Raphael. "Oh dear. Looks like Lucifer is throwing a hissy fit."

"It's because of me," said Thutmose. "I'm going to him." He stepped forward.

Metatron went to grab him, but just as he did Michael turned and put up his hand. A powerful energy pulse knocked Thutmose backwards, reeling into Raguel who caught him. "Bad move, Thutmose. Do *not* do that again," said Raguel.

Michael turned back to Lucifer, and Lucifer had turned grey. "You stopped him, Michael. I'm his father and you stopped him. You have still chosen the wrong side, Michael. He belongs to me. It was obvious he wanted to come to me and you stopped him." Lucifer began breathing heavily.

"Lucifer, stop it, we need to talk," said Michael.

"Step away, Michael," said Lucifer. He began to shake and his bones began to show through. He began to yowl and stretch like an animal. He was distorting with ugly teeth and the body was becoming black and grey. His eyes were almost popping, pointed ears flipped backwards, and a long snout stretched forward. There was a stink you could bottle and sell to knock out an army.

Michael ran back to the group. "He seems slightly annoyed," said Metatron.

Michael smiled briefly and put his hand on his sword. "It begins," said Michael.

"Oh, hell," said Jophiel.

"Yes," said Zadkiel, "all of them, I think."

Thutmose went towards Michael. "Get behind me, Thutmose," said Michael.

"Michael?" said Thutmose.

"Behind, NOW!" said Michael.

Metatron glanced. Michael was worried. Then there was a rush of dust and wind and the armies disappeared in a thick cloud.

CHAPTER 20

There were devils, demons and dwarves moving in and out of the cloud, and the Hell Dragons were picking off anyone they could. They couldn't get near the angels due to their huge size and stretch. Hell Dragons were more lethal for those with less height. Michael was swiping and swirling his sword around, catching anything that moved. He could hear calls of pain as the battle got under way. He couldn't see Lucifer, though. Where was he? He could feel someone behind him, but the energy told him it was Thutmose.

Thutmose was fighting confidently. He had already come across the dwarves before so he knew how to deal with them. It was tiring but he was doing well. He was throwing balls of fire at Hell Dragons if they swooped in too close and they scattered into ashes. Having been taught by Metatron, the size of the fireballs were only limited by Thutmose's mind alone. Thutmose saw Tutankhamen riding in and out of view, getting his wheels full of dwarves, then the next minute there were clear 'whoo-hoos' ringing through the air when he passed close by, with bits of fur, eyeballs and flesh spitting all over the desert sand.

Michael knew that Lucifer had the ability to cloak, so it made it difficult to sense him. The angels were making great strides cutting through Lucifer's army but they knew that these frontline demons were just fodder. Bruharis was fighting anything from Hell that came close enough to him and when it was clear, he flew high to find someone to fight and dodged spears and arrows. *He has the heart of a lion,* thought Michael.

Bruharis came in close to Thutmose and the two fought strongly together. As they were fighting, they were about to be attacked from behind by two demons. They turned just in time to see them approaching, but out of nowhere came Seth. Before Bruharis and Thutmose could react, they watched as Seth despatched both demons in a bloody pulpy mess. Seth turned and looked at Bruharis. He put his hand up in salute and ploughed into the fray.

"Bloody hell," said Bruharis and Thutmose in unison.

"My dad just saved my life," said Bruharis. "I really will have to say thank you to him one day, if he stays still long enough. It's not the first time." They laughed and returned to battle.

Lucifer was slinking through the army and killing anyone and anything that stood in his way, including those who were fighting on his side. Everyone and everything was dispensable. He was obsessed with getting to Thutmose and he knew where he was. Lucifer passed by Bes who was battling for his life and considered eating him, but knew he would suffer hugely, and anyway, the likes of Bes didn't taste particularly nice and if you were slow eating them, they fought their way out of your throat or stomach, depending which bits you hadn't chewed properly. Egyptian gods didn't like other Egyptian gods getting injured. They would rather injure each other; it was an Egyptian thing.

He was getting closer to Thutmose, then he thought he was in a fog.

"Well, who do we have here?"

Lucifer put his head back and closed his eyes. "Oh for goodness' sake, woman, don't you ever know when you have lost?"

Iside smiled. "I never lose, Lucifer, I just get even." She slung a ball of fire at him and Lucifer laughed as he swatted it away.

"Stupidity is a vile trait," he said. "I live with fire, but it makes it easier to kill you."

"Oh, that was a warmup," hissed Iside. "It will make this stick better..." And there it was, tar was stuck all over his wings. Lucifer howled and it echoed around the battle ground. He flew towards Iside and tried to grab her. She side stepped and kept out of his reach, disappearing and then reappearing. She was reciting Aganewta, the spell of the dead. He would be in another dimension in minutes.

The ground began to shake and the sand began to rise. "Well hello again," said a female voice. "Lucifer, how are you?" Serqet had burst out of the ground into the hugest black scorpion anyone had seen. People around her gave her space and some of Lucifer's army ran off, not wanting to get stung. She clipped her claws at him. "Need a haircut?" Lucifer tried to side step her but she grabbed him and pinned him down. "How rude," she laughed. "I haven't seen you in a long time, and you couldn't even be bothered to say hello?"

"Let me go, Serqet," Lucifer snapped, "or I'll snap off your leg and eat it."

Serqet used her other claw to help her pick Lucifer up, then she threw him against the rocks. She ran after him. Lucifer righted himself and she pinned him down again. She picked him up and threw him even harder. A Hell Dragon flew in and Serqet lifted a claw and cut its head off. It plunged to the floor, crushing a handful of dwarves. Serqet continued her onslaught of Lucifer. She was snipping and snapping at him, and Lucifer was dodging her tail. Lucifer twisted and turned and kept moving out of her grasp. Swinging with his sword, Lucifer caught her with a clear swipe, slicing off her front claw. There was a huge guttural scream and she changed into a goddess with part of her left arm missing. It distracted Iside long enough to stop her finishing the spell. Lucifer wanted to finish them both off, stupid women, but he did not have the time; he needed to put his plan into action.

Serqet screamed and threw the liquid from her arm towards Lucifer; it burned his back, but he kept moving away from her. The pain was agonising, but she would repair quickly. What was the point of being a goddess if you couldn't look after yourself? Now she knew how Lucifer moved and what to expect, next time they clashed, it would be different. Iside put up her hand towards Lucifer to finish the spell, and suddenly she was gone. A Hell Dragon had seen her and moved by Lucifer's mind, it picked Iside up, flying her away from the battlefield. Iside threw a fireball at the Hell Dragon as she swung precariously from its claw. As it dispersed, it dropped her, knocking her out cold.

Lucifer moved on, keeping on the outskirts of the battle. Anything or anyone who got in his way was destroyed. Everyone and everything was expendable.

His eyes were darting about and his sense of smell was getting stronger. He began to get excited. Thutmose was close; he was salivating just thinking about him. All that energy, all that power. He moved quicker and quicker and a short distance away, he saw Thutmose and standing close by was Michael. Lucifer was going to put his plan into action. He needed to get Thutmose away from Michael and he had the perfect solution but he would need to move quickly.

Lucifer planned to change into Michael and lure Thutmose away from the safety of Michael's protection. He would need to have Michael distracted to give him that time gap. Lucifer would persuade Thutmose to leave a doppelganger on view, so people would think he was still fighting, and would then slip into the dark dimension with Thutmose in tow, where he would drain him completely and take him back to Hell. He drew closer and closer to Thutmose and then felt a hand on his shoulder. "Hello, Luci. Going anywhere interesting?"

He looked up into the face of Raphael. "Oh, for goodness' sake, Raphael, go away and play with the other angels."

Raphael smiled. "Fighting talk, eh Luci? Come on then, let's get on with it."

"Decided to get up off your backside instead of sitting at the right hand of our father, eh Raphael? About time you did something for your place that you so happily stole off the rest of us."

"Oh, Lucifer, you are making my heart cry. No one took anything from you that you didn't deserve to have taken. You did this to yourself." Raphael drew his sword. "Of course, I could just cut your head off right here, but I think our father would prefer you had a chance."

Lucifer rose to his full angelic glory. His wings were outstretched, strong and powerful. "Don't try me, Raphael. You don't know who you are playing with."

"Oh, this is no play, Lucifer," Raphael smiled, "this is something you have caused, yet again, and refuse to take responsibility for. You think everyone and everything belongs to you, and we are here to teach you a lesson you will never forget."

"Never is a very long time, Raphael," Lucifer sneered, and battle commenced.

The battle was fast and furious and Lucifer was conscious of how little time he had left. He had to get away from Raphael; fighting with him was futile. Lucifer suddenly vanished. Raphael didn't have Michael's knowledge of Lucifer so still swung his sword around in case he came within close proximity. Eventually he realised Lucifer was gone. "OK," he said to himself. "Scared him off… well done, Raph," then he went deeper into the battle looking for a fight. Closing his eyes, Lucifer beseeched Azazel to rise from Hell to distract Michael by fighting with him. In the midst of all the chaos, it was likely that Michael would, at least for a few short seconds, lose his connection with Thutmose. Lucifer would then fly in masquerading as Michael and take Thutmose. He would tell Thutmose to quickly release his doppelganger to fool Lucifer, ensuring there would be no struggle and an easy escape. Thutmose's doppelganger would keep everyone fooled at least until the angels noticed he was really missing, then it would be too late.

Lucifer's plan came to fruition. Azazel, being allowed by Lucifer to take solid form once in a thousand years, appeared in front of Michael and drew his sword. Split seconds was all it took; Michael flew to meet Azazel and Lucifer swooped in and took Thutmose. The battle between Azazel and Michael was brief. Azazel had played his part and besides, he did not wish to fight, his heart really was not in it these days. No sooner had the fight begun, then Azazel, putting his sword to his forehead and bowing down, suddenly disappeared. Michael, feeling confused, spun around. He could still see Thutmose fighting next to Bruharis but something was terribly wrong. He stopped and looked at the structure of Thutmose's body and realised it was most certainly not Thutmose – it was his doppelganger. Michael looked around, wondering if Thutmose had done this purposefully. Was he injured? Did he need help? Was he trying to confuse the enemy? He looked up into the sky and knew his answer. God relayed to him that Lucifer had indeed taken Thutmose but he was not to intervene. This was the final confrontation to decide Thutmose's soul. If Thutmose changed sides, all would be destroyed by God.

Michael was devastated. Metatron flew to him above the noise of the battle and shouted. "He's gone?"

"Yes," said Michael, "and it's up to Thutmose now."

Bruharis looked confused then dropped his sword hand. "Michael, I'm sorry, I'm so sorry. I thought you had come to take him. I couldn't hear properly what was being said, but I thought he was in danger, I just kept fighting."

Michael put his hand on Bruharis' shoulder. "It's find, Bru, don't worry, we'll find him."

Bruharis sheathed his sword. "No, he was fighting with me, I'll find him. Our fathers are angels of death, I'll find him." ...And he took to the air.

Michael shouted, "Bru, no!" but it was too late, he was gone.

CHAPTER 21

Thutmose was flying with Michael but then he realised something was not right. He knew from the smell permeating his nostrils. He looked up and stared into the face of Lucifer. Lucifer seemed to be looking through Thutmose. His speed was breathtaking and before Thutmose knew it, they were swiftly inside a gloomy dark dimension. Lucifer set Thutmose down and disappeared into the darkness. There was complete silence. Thutmose could see in the darkness; his eyes adjusted like the vision of a cat. He remembered Bruharis' training. Thutmose put his head down and closed his eyes. He concentrated and let the sense of the atmosphere around him fill his mind and his body. He knew that Lucifer had brought him here for a purpose and he knew what that purpose was. He lifted his head and stared at Lucifer who was a distance away.

"I can see you, Lucifer."

"Well, where did I hear that not so long ago? Oh yes, some old lady out in the desert who was trying to ruin my eternity." Lucifer planted the vision inside Thutmose's head and he saw the exchange that had taken place between Lucifer and Iside. He felt deep sorrow as he saw an image of her on a hillside, her eyes closed. Lucifer squinted his eyes, reading Thutmose's emotions. "She's dead, of course," Lucifer said, and smirked at the visible pain that crossed

Thutmose face.

"I've been looking for you for a long time, Lucifer."

Lucifer was slightly irritated that Thutmose was not calling him 'Father', but he let that go.

"I've always been close by. I've watched every move you have made over the millennia. You were never very creative with your life, though, were you? Your immortal life really has been meaningless. You could have had, done and been anything you wanted, but rather than live your life, you have mourned it. You don't really deserve to have what I gave you. What a waste. There are people who are far more worthy than you. If I was God I would have destroyed you on the spot and taken all that energy and given it to the likes of bloody Noah. Of all the people in all the world who could have made use of thousands of years of life, it fell to you. What a sad day for the world that was."

"What you gave me?" Thutmose began to move forward. "You gave me nothing except a scar marking me as your son. I grew up in a village where people despised me. I had to leave the village because people knew who I was. My step-father beat me and made my life miserable, and I have been alone because of this position you have put me in. I could not live a normal human life because of you. Everything you are, has made me who I am. The misery, the anger, the sorrow, the pain, the loneliness, it's all because of you. I have never been a whole person. But now... Luci, the angels and Egyptian gods have taught me who I want to be and they are my friends."

Lucifer was smarting at the 'Luci' quip. "Oh, boo-hoo," said Lucifer, rubbing his eyes like a child. "So you think they are your friends? They are not your friends. Do you honestly think that I could have taken you so easily if they didn't want you to be removed from the battle? They let me take you. The battle was merely a smoke screen. We all got together and had a chat, and decided to go ahead with this farcical scuffle just to make you think you were important, at least to someone. You were drawn in so easily by the whole façade. Michael knew I was on my way and he also knew you wouldn't leave with me in my own skin, so I had to humiliate myself by turning into Michael, so you would come with me. What do you think we were discussing before the battle when Michael stood in front of me? We were laughing at you. Finalising our plans. The battle is, in fact, over now and everyone has gone back to doing what they will continue to do for an eternity, finally happy to get away from whining, crying, whingeing Thutmose, who is so boring that dead bodies are more interesting than him. Still, it was a nice little game we all played. Sometimes you just have to get out of the rat race and have a bit of fun. So, we played with you and what fun we all had. Don't believe me? Look." Lucifer swept his hand up in the air and a vision appeared. The battleground was clear. Bruharis and the Egyptian gods were saying goodbye. One by one they shook hands and left the battlefield.

Thutmose could hear their voices, the laughing and joking and Jophiel saying to Michael, "I'll bet Thutmose will never speak to you again."

Tutankhamen was laughing and shouting to the other gods, "Well, it looks like I'm going to have to hide for another four thousand years." The laughter rang in Thutmose's ears. Lucifer swept his arm up again and the vision disappeared.

"If I had left you on that battlefield, my father, who art in

Heaven, would have struck you down. You are a liability and they cannot afford to have two of us running the dungeons." Lucifer saw the pain flick across Thutmose's face and he felt a true sense of amusement.

Thutmose swallowed; his stomach felt like it was turning over. Was it true? Had he really just seen everyone leaving the battlefield? Was it truly a game? Had he been left alone?

"Come here, come to Daddy. Let me end your complete and utterly miserable life. I'll extract the energy and before you know it, it will all be over."

Lucifer started towards Thutmose, but Thutmose put up his hand. "No." Lucifer stopped. He felt the strength flowing in Thutmose's body. He would have to tear him apart to take the energy out. He had not really wanted to go that far; he hated mess. He could, however, play along a little longer. "Do you need more proof?"

Thutmose looked at Lucifer. "Did you ever love me, Lucifer?"

At that moment, Lucifer felt the spark of love given to him when he was created by God. He changed into the angel he truly was and his radiance shone. Thutmose was taken aback, his eyes filled with tears as he stared at Lucifer. He was in awe. "You are beautiful."

Lucifer smiled. "I know, I hear it all the time." His laughter rang out like golden bells and it was so infectious, Thutmose laughed too. Then there was silence. "Yes, I have loved you and I do love you. After all, you are my son. I just want what is best for you."

Thutmose moved a little way away from Lucifer. There was a feeling he could not shake. Lucifer narrowed his eyes, but stayed where he was, watching Thutmose like a cat watches a mouse. "I've tried to find you on several occasions, father," Thutmose was looking at his fingers like a child now, "but every time I thought I was close, you would disappear."

"Well let's just say my father gave me orders to leave you be, so I couldn't just come and visit. It would have been the end of me and unlike you, I quite like my immortality. I know why you have been searching for me, Thutmose, and I can give you the answer if it is truly what you want to hear, but remember, when you choose, there is no going back."

"I know, Father, and I'm certain I want to know the answer."

Lucifer felt uncomfortable that Thutmose was now calling him 'Father', but he said nothing.

Lucifer created a seating position. "You were very small when you were born, you know, and when your mother died after giving birth to you, Gabriel came to fetch her. I remember watching her leave through the window and when I turned around, there you were. I could hardly contain my excitement at this beautiful child I had created with your mother. I stood over your cot whilst you slept and stayed with you until the first sunrise of your life. I couldn't stay any longer because of your father returning from the party he went to, celebrating your birth. I have watched you with love and care over the millennia and there have been many times I have wanted to intervene, to help you, to make life happier for you, but for some reason, I've never got it quite right." Lucifer smirked at the lie he was so liberally pouring over Thutmose. He was watching Thutmose as the energy began to glow with joy inside him. Lucifer was getting twitchy; he needed that energy, it was like it was singing to him, calling him forward. He really wasn't enjoying this family moments session.

"I always wanted a natural life for you, Thutmose, one where you would be loved by someone, someone who would accept you for who you were and who would take care of you. I even wanted you to have a little Thutmose. You would have been a good father, Thutmose. You have learned from the upbringing you have had."

"Yes, I would have," he said.

Lucifer sighed and walked closer to Thutmose. "Have you never been in love?"

"I think you know the answer to that, Father."

Lucifer looked at his nails in the brightness of his wings. "No, I really don't. It's a family thing, you see. I cannot tell what you are thinking, even if you think I can. If I wanted to know, I would have to rip your head off and eat your brain." Thutmose looked startled. "Oh, I'm not going to, don't worry." *But I will if I have to,* he thought.

Thutmose turned his back. Lucifer thought about attacking him when suddenly Thutmose said, "I thought I was in love, once, many years ago in London. Her interest finished pretty quickly when I levitated above my bed. So I ended up being alone again."

Of course, Lucifer knew this because the levitation was in fact down to him and his jealousy. He was in the darkness and found it funny when the lady concerned fled the premises. Lucifer had subsequently watched the emotional pain that Thutmose had gone through with a very joyful heart. Perhaps he could get Thutmose to commit suicide, two jobs with one blow, energy transference and the soul of his son to torture for eternity.

"It's about emotion," said Lucifer. "It's about letting go. You need to have truly decided that life is no longer for you.

You cut ties with every memory you have ever made, you decide that it is time to fall, but you really have to mean it, you have to feel it in every part of your being. You say goodbye to everyone who knows you, to every acquaintance you have ever made. You say goodbye to family, friends, your property, etc., etc., and once you have detached yourself from it all, you close your eyes and fall."

"Fall from where?"

"You fall off a cliff." Lucifer looked at Thutmose, slightly confused. "You're a god. You won't feel anything, you would have disposed of all your natural feelings and when you hit the ground, it will be over. You wouldn't have felt a thing. Your body closes off on the way down. Your spirit, realising it is no longer of any use, leaves the carcass before it hits the floor. Look, I'm sorry, Thutmose, but Michael would have told you this surely when you were in training?"

Thutmose thought of Michael and the pain shot through him. He thought he was his friend. "No, he didn't tell me anything about it, I just knew what happened if your doppelganger jumped."

Lucifer turned away, smirking. If Thutmose cut ties with everything and jumped, his soul would end up in Hell. God wouldn't want him. He knew he had Thutmose almost where he wanted him. "You just can't trust anyone these days." The lies rolled off Lucifer's tongue too easily. He could barely contain his laughter.

Thutmose knew that he was just playing for time now. He looked at Lucifer and could not understand why this had happened to him. His life story to any mortal would seem so incredible they would not believe him.

"It's just the luck of the draw," said Lucifer.

Thutmose frowned. "What do you mean?"

"Oh, you just opened your mind for a second there and I heard what you said. Your mother, well, she could have been anyone. It was just this time, it was your mother. She was incredibly beautiful, you know, and we had fallen, and God was angry. We were angry, and she was just so beautiful."

Thutmose was stunned. "So you took my mother without her consent?"

"Of course not. What do you think I am? As far as your mother was concerned, I was your father, so she did consent."

"So, you fooled her into thinking you were my biological father?"

"Gods do it all the time," said Lucifer. "Look at Zeus."

Thutmose could feel his anger welling up inside him. "No, don't let's look at Zeus, let's look at what you did."

Lucifer was beginning to get angry too. It was one thing having to steal his own son, but it was quite another being questioned as to exactly why he had come into being. "Oh for goodness' sake!" shrieked Lucifer. "It was thousands and thousands of years ago. There were many human women taken by Watchers, just thank your lucky stars you weren't born a Nephilim, you would have had God chasing you from one end of the earth to another, then he would have tried to drown you in a flood and to top it all, he would have sent some little squirt with a slingshot to kill you. Instead, you have lived a long life that you have completely wasted and should never have belonged to you in the first place. So no, we won't look at me and what I have done, but I will look at you inside bloody out, now come here."

Lucifer ran towards Thutmose and was completely taken

unawares. Thutmose somersaulted out of the way and punched Lucifer straight in his face, knocking him quite a distance. Thutmose disappeared and cloaked. He watched Lucifer and realised he was now playing on very unequal ground.

Lucifer knew this game because he invented it. Thutmose was his son and he knew exactly where he was – the cloaking came from Lucifer. "God will kill you, Thutmose, if you leave here without me. The archangels were told to get close to you to find out what your weaknesses are. You have done some bad things in your life, Thutmose, and only I can save you."

Thutmose stayed still; Lucifer strode towards him with long meaningful strides. He reached out and grabbed Thutmose. "You pathetic little parasite. This is my ground, my kingdom, my dimension. How dare you try to take control?" And he threw Thutmose with such force, that when he hit the ground, it broke his arm with a resounding crack. Thutmose doubled in pain; it felt like he had been hit full force with a lightning bolt.

Lucifer strode towards him again. He picked him up and threw him a second time; the arm cracked again. Lucifer was becoming more and more angry and beginning to enjoy himself. The more he hurt Thutmose, the more he wanted to hurt him. He picked Thutmose up and threw him again and Thutmose hit the ground hard. "I'm going to kill you, and I don't care what God thinks." Lucifer, unable to control his excitement had transformed into a half demon and was screaming. A wailing sound was emitting from his throat and a laughter that sounded like a thousand people being tortured. Thutmose could not get up. Lucifer ran towards him and as he reached for him, there was a flash of light and Bruharis flew into Lucifer's path. "No!" he shouted.

Knocked off guard, Lucifer righted himself within seconds. Bruharis had Thutmose in his arms. Thutmose smiled weakly at Bruharis who just as he was about to exit the dark dimension, missed Lucifer coming in from his left. The dimension split open and Bruharis, or what was left of him, hit the ground and Thutmose rolled in the sand towards Jophiel. The battle was ending; the archangels and the gods had clearly won. A wind was blowing and it seemed to be clearing the area of the visitors from Hell.

Lucifer was seething; he was breathing heavily. He threw Bruharis' arms down on the floor and turned to disappear back towards Hell. He suddenly stopped and sniffed the air. "Oh no." he had just registered that he had killed Seth's son. "Oh well." He turned his back and disappeared.

The gods and angels stood for a minute and Seth stepped forward. Jophiel had taken Thutmose a safe distance from Bruharis. Thutmose was in so much pain, it was better for him not see Bruharis while they decided what to do about the whole situation. Michael looked up to the sky, but God was silent.

CHAPTER 22

God stood and looked at Lucifer and Lucifer stared straight back. "What? What?" His wings outstretched. "I am what you made me. Did you honestly think any of this was going to end well? In fact, you knew it wouldn't end well but you let it go ahead anyway. You had every chance to intervene and you didn't. So, is this the end now? Are you going to completely wipe me out?" God said nothing. "Oh, Father, please don't hurt me, please tell me you forgive me and the slate is wiped clean. Oh boo-hoo, oh boo-hoo. I kept away like you told me to, but you just had to let them dangle a carrot, didn't you? Did you do it on purpose? Maybe you did it for kicks?" Still, God said nothing, he just listened. "He was my son, and he was serving a purpose, the purpose was…?" Lucifer held his hand out for God to finish the sentence. "Will you just stop this silent treatment?" And still, God said nothing. Lucifer rattled on and on about having been left outside of Heaven, the fact he was God's first archangel, the fact that nobody loved him anymore. The Watchers, history, and after hours of shouting, screaming and crying, flitting from devil to demon and eventually back to the angel God first created. He went silent apart from his panting from exhaustion.

God finally spoke. "You were my favourite, Lucifer. I was so proud of you. You were quick, clever, intelligent, witty, loving and compassionate. I never believed that I could have created someone so pure, clean and so strong as you. You encompassed everything that an archangel should truly be. You were my right hand, Lucifer, but you just had to go that one step further and try to oust me. I have listened to you and everything you say is true, but only in your eyes. You have become selfish, brutish, spiteful, unforgiving and you have embraced every evil and debasement known to mankind. The angel I see before me now is just a mirage."

God swept his hand over Lucifer and before him was a hideous horned demon.

"You have never asked for true forgiveness, Lucifer, and you have turned your back on mankind and on me. You chose the eternity that you now have and whilst it is true, I could end you in a breath, I will not, at least not yet. You are cursed, Lucifer, and now until I choose to close down all the stars and fold the universe in on itself, you will be this that is before me now. Anything you create will be a mirage and I will ensure that you never see Michael again, unless in battle, and if you dare to step foot in Heaven, I will destroy you. I know you will not come to Heaven, Lucifer, because despite yourself, you enjoy your immortality and all the things it brings you. The stench of the ages will be with you forever, Lucifer. The cries and bewilderments of those you have corrupted will be your companions for eternity. Your time is nearly over, Lucifer, your end will come naturally as mankind turns to me and rests with me forever. I am sorry for you, Lucifer; I am sorry that you have never found your way back to me and back to your family. I can see that your evil soul will always battle. You may have small victories, but I will have the overall victory. Your end is nigh, Lucifer."

Lucifer took in the magnitude of what God had said. He could cope with anything, but not the loss of Michael. "Michael won't listen to you, Father, we are one."

"No, no you are not," said God. "Michael is my son and he will do as I ask. Goodbye, Lucifer. Time will move swiftly, I'm sure." God disappeared.

Lucifer ran about like a confused rat in a maze. "No, Father, no, wait, let me speak." But it was too late. He was left with the buzzing and filth and screams of all he had collected over the millennia. Lucifer started to become hysterical and suddenly a thunderstorm so severe and enormous began and he screamed so loud, it could be heard over the thunder.

Michael and Metatron looked at each other. God had conversed with them both. "Michael, I'm sorry," said Metatron.

"Doesn't matter, serves him right," said Michael. "We need to help Thutmose."

Geb and Horus picked Thutmose up and took him towards Abu Simbel. He was sleeping under the energy imposed on him by the angels. The earth shook slightly and Seth appeared. He was enraged, but trying to remain calm. "Where is Lucifer?"

Michael and Metatron looked at each other. "He's in Hell, literally," said Metatron. "He has just had a very long discussion with our father and it didn't end well."

Seth glared, holding Bruharis limp and mangled body in his arms. "Lucifer will be having a very long discussion with me. He dared to kill my son and as long as we inhabit the same dimensions, he will have no peace." Seth disappeared, taking Bruharis with him.

Geb and Horus took their places by Thutmose's body. Geb stood at his head and Horus stood at his feet. "Lucifer must have been in an uncontrollable rage to have done such damage to Thutmose. He could have crippled him for centuries, but if Thutmose wants to leave this world, we need to be certain that it is what he wants," Horus whispered. Geb and Horus raised their hands over Thutmose's body. The light was blinding as Geb and Horus took him away. This god would be taken to the 'Children of Horus' who were Amset, Hapi, Tuamãutef and Qebehsenuef, in the Abode of the Blessed. When they reached the gateway, they were met by Maat, the wife of Thoth and daughter of Ra. She was a very ancient goddess and knew all that there was to know about Thutmose. She accepted him into the dimension of that she resided in and the gods left Thutmose to decide his fate.

Maat waited whilst Thutmose's spirit exited his body. He raised himself up as though from a night's sleep. He sat very still, taking in his surroundings. He saw Maat and knew instantly who she was. "Am I asleep?" Maat looked on. "Am I dead?"

Maat spoke to him. "No, you are not dead and you do not need to use your voice." She smiled.

"So are you telepathic?"

Maat stood up. "The whole of mankind is telepathic, Thutmose, but it was a skill lost many millennia ago. Only the gods use it now. Sometimes people stumble upon it, but use it incorrectly, trying to alter it or use it for invasiveness."

"What has happened to me?"

Maat pointed to his body. "You have been damaged." Thutmose stumbled; he had not realised that he had left his body. "The damage is severe, so you have been brought here to be weighed, measured and if you are found to be wanting, you will be sent to Limbo where you will walk for a thousand years. I will be taking you to my father, Ra."

Thutmose suddenly began to panic. As an Egyptian he knew what confrontation with Ra would bring and he felt it would be worse than with his father. "You will need to make things right. You should be true, tell the truth, be real, genuine, upright, righteous, just steadfast and wholly unalterable. Should you fail on any of these points, then you will be removed to Limbo. You will need a Champion. Who do you choose?"

Thutmose thought about all those who had gone before him, and wished that Bruharis were here.

"I hear your choice and you have chosen well." Thutmose frowned; he had not expressed his desire out loud. Maat disappeared; he was alone.

He walked over to his body and viewed the damage. The bones in his arms were protruding in all sorts of positions and he felt sorrow for the body lying there. He felt that his father must have really hated him to inflict such injuries. The scene repeated in his head. It was as though he were watching someone else, but he still felt the brutal attack as he watched the body being flung about as though it were a branch in a storm. He reflected on his passion to leave an immortal life, but felt that having met his friend Bruharis, he could achieve much, but only if he was given a second chance.

"Completely agree," said a voice and laughter rang out that filled the heaven of Maat. Bruharis charged forward to meet his friend.

Thutmose was taken aback. "What are you doing here?"

Bruharis smiled. "Your father killed me."

"But you can't die, you are a god like me."

"Well it appears we have our weaknesses," laughed Bruharis, "and I guess being torn limb from limb by your father, is mine."

Thutmose was shocked. He didn't know how Bruharis could joke about something so dreadful. He had literally given his life to save Thutmose and now Thutmose was fighting for that life. He didn't know what to say. Bruharis held out his hand and Thutmose took it. The next moment they were in ancient Abu Simbel where Thutmose had first met Bruharis. "No one can see us," smiled Bruharis. "We can walk anywhere we want to, but the really good thing about it is that we can eat and drink as much as we like and it won't affect us, but it's great fun, come on. We have much to talk about, your judgement is pending."

Seth strode into Hell as though he owned the place. Lucifer raised his head up from his seat and his lips drew backwards. He sniffed the air around him. "Seth," he muttered. He stood up and began to run towards the smell. Seth felt movement and began to run towards the vibration. The ground in Hell began to shake and an earthquake began on Earth. At first it was a mild shudder but it would increase in intensity when the gods collided head on. Lucifer knew exactly where Seth was in his kingdom.

Seth was at a disadvantage, having never ventured into Hell before. Lucifer flew around the back of Seth, landing on him and knocking him to the ground. Lucifer pummelled his head until it was a bloody mess. He stood up, breathing heavily. Looking away, he contemplated where to put Seth, when just as he turned around, he felt a huge fist punch him in the face and knock him flying into the rocks. Dazed, he was too late to push Seth, who was bashing his head into the rocks, off him. Lucifer put his arms out and tried to push but Seth hung on. The beating Lucifer suffered was brutal, and he began to laugh. Seth stopped long enough for Lucifer to grab him by his head and swing him around and around at such speed, that when he let go, Seth smashed into the ground.

Lucifer was seething and walked towards Seth to finish him. Seth rose back up just as Lucifer reached him. He tore into Lucifer, ripping pieces of his wings off, and with a wail of pain, Lucifer turned into the dragon. He shot fire at Seth who ran over rock after rock as Lucifer meant to burn him. Seth stood on the top of the rocks and waited. Lucifer shot fire at him and then Seth was gone. Lucifer became very still, and closed his eyes. He knew Seth was still around somewhere, he had merely transfigured into something else.

Lucifer opened his eyes and saw in the darkness, the figure of Seth slowly approaching. Lucifer sniggered; this was too easy. He crawled towards Seth. Lucifer opened his mouth and swallowed Seth whole. Lucifer tried to change back into his angelic form but couldn't; he was stuck. He tried and tried but was stuck fast.

Seth pushed his way out of Lucifer's stomach. "C'mon, Luci, if I can climb out of my mother's womb before I'm fully formed, I can get out of your stomach, no problem, and that little change you are struggling with? Well, that's a gift from me. You see, I know what you know and by swallowing me, you took a little bit of me that I decided to leave with you."

Lucifer went wild. He thrashed and struggled and screamed. Seth just stood watching, then Lucifer turned into Seth. "Now that's what I call handsome," laughed Seth, then he punched Lucifer in the face and once again sent him flying into the rocks.

Lucifer stood up and all sense of fairness had left him. The battle between the two became extremely violent. They smashed each other, they threw each other; one minute Seth was winning and the next, Lucifer. The ground began to suffer an earthquake. Rocks, sand, dust, gravel, dirt all of it fell on top of them. Dark clouds moved across the sun. Ice began to form on the sand. Sharp winds were blowing and the clouds swirled like dancers in a frenzy. The gods were watching and were disturbed by what they saw. They agreed to intervene and restrain both Lucifer and Seth if the fighting did not cease. But suddenly, the fight was over and the shuddering stopped.

Lucifer was sitting on the floor, his wings outstretched, torn and bloody. Large open gashes showed on his body. Seth was bleeding heavily from wounds in his arms and legs, and Lucifer had bitten an ear off.

"I'm bored of this now," said Lucifer. Seth said nothing. "I killed your son by accident. I was actually trying to kill my son, but Bruharis got in the way."

"Why would you kill your own son?" said Seth. "I've heard the rumours, but what you want is pointless, your father could take it away from you in seconds."

Lucifer leaned his head back on his wings and stretched out his legs. "I know, but I'm Lucifer, I always want things that I can't or am not supposed to have, it's a challenge."

"Like Michael?"

Lucifer looked up. "Well it doesn't matter now; our father says I have to stay away from him."

"But you won't?"

"If I don't our father will finish me, and I haven't got long now anyway. No one seems to want me around anymore."

Seth stood up. "You are unbelievably stupid, Lucifer. You could have had Heaven on Earth if you had just given yourself time to think and stopped being so impulsive. Why would you try to battle someone who you simply cannot beat in any way? He was your creator, your father, it was preordained he could destroy you too." Seth dusted himself off. Lucifer turned around. "Where are you going?"

"I'm leaving to get my son."

Lucifer stood up. He shook himself clean and suddenly materialised into the angel God had created.

Seth smiled. "You are exceptionally beautiful, Lucifer."

"Yes, I know, everyone tells me, but no one seems to love me for long."

"I can understand what Michael saw in you."

"Still does, if only he would admit it," sighed Lucifer. "Do you want your ear back? I can regurgitate it if you like? Bit of a party trick."

"Er, no thanks," said Seth. "I'm a god. Plenty more where they came from." Seth flicked the damaged ear and it was perfect.

"Thanks for an entertaining few hours," shouted Lucifer as Seth began to leave. Seth kept walking and eventually disappeared. "So rude," said Lucifer. He picked himself up, dusted himself off, and changed back into a demon. He really was not feeling the slightest bit angelic today. "That was a mistake, Seth," he whispered.

CHAPTER 23

Thutmose stood silently in front of Ra. Ra stared at him; he was unimpressed with Thutmose and was already considering him for Limbo. Maat broke into his thoughts. "Father, give him a chance."

Ra stood up and walked around Thutmose. He walked over to his battered and damaged body and saw the destruction that Lucifer had wrought upon it. He looked towards Thutmose and asked, "What is your first memory?"

Thutmose looked at Bruharis and Maat. Maat nodded her head. "A pain on my left cheek when I was in my cot."

Ra smiled. "I meant your first memory of being active in life?"

Thutmose was standing with his hands behind his back. He felt like a child at school. Ra was waiting. "My father beating me and blaming me for my mother's death. He told me I was a bastard and had ruined their lives, he said the sooner I was gone the better, he said I should have died when I was born."

Ra showed no emotion. "How did that make you feel?"

"I felt like I was nobody, I felt useless, I was afraid of him and it made me afraid of people. I had no confidence." Ra said nothing. Thutmose felt he was waiting for him to continue. "So as I got older…"

Ra held up his hand; he was looking thoughtful. "What did

you think you could bring to the world?"

"I don't know."

Ra stood and looked at Thutmose and frowned. "You don't know?"

Bruharis was putting his hands up to his eyes and his head back, like he wanted to scream. Maat put her hand on Bruharis arm and smiled. "Think harder," said Ra. There was a sharpness to his voice. "You are being weighed and measured. If you are found wanting…"

"I know, I know…" Thutmose said. "I'm, I'm thoughtful, I'm considerate, I'm compassionate…"

"Well," said Ra, striding towards him, "I think if I tore your heart out now and weighed it against Maat's feather, your heart would go crashing through every dimension there is."

Thutmose took a step back. "No, please."

Ra stopped. "I ask you again, what can you bring to this world of immortals? Why do you think I should allow you to remain, you, the one who has mourned his immorality for millennia, you who has, from what you are saying, done nothing of consequence. Am I right? You who has chased his father, only to meet him in combat and ended up here in front of me? What can you offer the world of immortals that we don't already have?"

The children of Horus Amset, Hapi, Tuamãutef and Qebehsenuef emerged from the glowing white brightness that surrounded the court of Ra. They looked at Thutmose with disdain. They all spoke in unison. "Father, this so-called immortal god is of no use. It is time to forget him, let him go, he is not of any use to us here or on Earth. Erase him, make him nothing, as he considers he is. This is the egg he grew from."

Ra held up his hand. "We will give him the chance to show us who he is."

The children of Horus sighed in unison. Ra waited.

Thutmose bowed his head and closed his eyes. He remembered a fight in school, a boy in his class who was weak and fragile and was a sickly child. The boy's name was Ani and he was getting bullied by a much bigger boy who was also bigger than Thutmose. The bully's name was Cheuput; he had a face that was battered and scarred. He had been in many fights, but had always won. The children were scared of him. He did not intimidate Thutmose, though, there was something about Thutmose that frightened Cheuput. Thutmose saw Cheuput knocking Ani about and pushing him to the floor. Thutmose did not think about his own safety, and had intervened. Thutmose was given a bloody nose, but he beat the bigger boy almost to a bloody pulp for bullying Ani. Ani was never picked on again, and Thutmose was the class king. Sadly, Ani passed from his illness 10 years later. Thutmose was by his side and held his friend's hand because Ani was scared. Thutmose told him about wonderful things he would see when he met the angels. Thutmose did not know how he knew these things, but he did know they were true. He raised his head and looked at Ra. There were no signs of emotion on Ra's face. "Continue." Thutmose once again closed his eyes.

Thutmose remembered falling off a cliff when he was a young boy and his friend jumped after him. Thutmose would not give him up for dead and tried for two hours to revive his friend. His parents hadn't let Thutmose come to funeral; they had blamed him and said but for his showing off, their son would still be alive. They said he was the son of the devil and only a devil boy could have survived that fall. In the evening, he had attended the site of the burning of his friend and talked to him as though he were alive. He cried and apologised for not succeeding in reviving him. He slept by his friend's grave site all night.

Thutmose went through his life and a pattern had been created; he had always looked after his friends. The times he had been let down he had retained his sorrows inside. In ancient Egypt, he recalled looking after the old lady in the marketplace, making sure she was home safely. He recalled the sorrow at growing up with no mother, and only having met her when he died at the hands of Snefru. Finally, he recalled fighting with the angels in the battle for his soul. But this proved nothing. Then finally, he recalled the murder he had committed in his home and his intention to bury the body of a burglar so it would never be found. He raised his head and looked at Ra.

Ra walked towards Thutmose and looked at him thoughtfully. "Murder? You say you committed a murder?" Thutmose nodded his head. Ra told Thutmose to close his eyes and he put his hand on Thutmose head. When Ra removed his hand, Thutmose looked at him and his heart was pounding. "You did not commit murder, Thutmose. Rather it was your father."

Thutmose was confused. "But I thought…"

"You thought wrong, Thutmose. Your father possessed your body and put you in stasis long enough to remove the male from your house. You were going to your cellar for wine, not tools. Your true father must really hate you."

Thutmose became unsteady on his feet with shock. "I am so stupid, you're right." Thutmose said, "I have no right to an immortal life. People the world over do as I do – we are the same, me and them. I have been found wanting, you may take my heart."

Ra then raised his hand. Bruharis rushed forward. "No, please, no, my God Ra, please don't let him be erased; he doesn't know what he is saying."

Amset, Hapi, Tuamãutef and Qebehsenuef all spoke in unison. "Let him be erased, he is worth nothing, he is not worthy of the title 'God'. He is correct when he says he is the same as people the world over. Anyone would have done what he has done; he has done nothing special."

Ra looked at Bruharis and smiled. "I assure you, he does know what he is saying, Bru, because he is here with us. We cannot lie, we cannot hide. Any man is open to me and I can see deep inside his soul. Thutmose has never been settled as an immortal, he has always wanted the human things in life. He wanted to be a father, he wanted to marry, he wanted children. Instead, he has spent the majority of his immortal existence alone. Despite his own feelings, he has stepped in to help and save anyone who has needed him and I for one, would want to know that if I was in mortal danger, that there would be someone like Thutmose nearby to help me." Ra looked at Thutmose and put his hand on his shoulder. "I'm not taking you away, Thutmose, I am sending you back. You are without doubt, one of the kindest and most caring gods I have ever come across, but you also have the heart of the Sphinx. Don't look so sad. There are trials ahead, but you will come out of them. Immortal lives change in strange and supernatural ways. You have been given a very special gift, Thutmose. The mightiest of the mighty knows you and can help you if you let him in. You need to know your soul. In ancient Greece there is a doorway, crumbled now, but the words remain. Know thy self, Thutmose, you need to know who you truly are and use it. Your decision will come in time." Ra raised his hand. "Now be gone. I have things to do."

Ra shoved Thutmose extremely hard in his chest and he woke up aching from head to foot, on his bed in Paris. His injuries were healed and only aches remained where they had been. Thutmose sat up and watched the full moon outside. He realised that Bruharis had not come with him. His friend, who he had adopted as his brother; his friend who had given his life to save his. The friend who had stood by him in the court of Ra and begged Ra for his life. Thutmose heart cracked. The tears hot and heavy rolled down his face, and he sobbed as he had sobbed in Abu Simbel. In the darkness, the spirit of Azazel was quietly watching Thutmose's every move. Now Ra was on Thutmose's side, this could be very dangerous.

CHAPTER 24

"He what?"

"He was with Ra. Ra gave him a second chance and sent him back."

Lucifer was outraged. "And, Lucifer…" continued Azazel, "Thutmose knows it wasn't him who committed the murder."

Lucifer yelled a guttural yell. "Why is everyone interfering in my business? I have spent millennia doing what I do and no one has ever complained, now my son, my son on Earth no less, has grown up, he has gone completely the wrong way and is causing me problems. I've been there for him his whole life and got him out of so many scrapes, but has he ever thanked me? Has he ever told me he loves me? No! And what does he do in my presence? He prays to him, him, him, him, him." Lucifer was jabbing his finger at the sky. "Well I tell you now, Azazel, I'm not letting him get away with it."

Azazel frowned, but said nothing. He had always followed Lucifer and where had it got him? He knew he had no chance of redemption, but perhaps there was something he could do to help stop this continuous roundabout of trouble. "Lucifer, please don't go to Ra. I know it is what you are thinking, but if you do, you may not come back. Ra is different than Seth and he could destroy you just as our father can."

"He wouldn't dare." Lucifer, flicked his hand in the air. "I am the first born—"

Azazel interrupted. "We know, Lucifer, but Ra is dangerous. He sent Thutmose back…"

Lucifer walked up to Azazel, nose to nose. "I know all about Ra, Azazel, but if you interrupt me again, you will spend the rest of eternity as a spectre and I will never allow you to see the light of day." Then he was gone.

Azazel was angry. How dare he speak to him as though he were less than he? Azazel turned. "If I murdered Thutmose, I could have an extra thousand years, I could roam the world again." But as quickly as the thought was there, it was gone.

Lucifer strode into the court of Ra, completely unannounced. Ra rose from his throne and the children of Horus took a deep breath in. "Ta Ra, long time no see. How are things? Oh no, wait a minute, I didn't need to ask that question, because we all know what has been happening."

Ra looked towards Maat who could do nothing except shrug.

"Knock-knock. Ra baby, I'm coming in."

Ra stopped him immediately. He closed his mind and spoke. "Lucifer, you should not be here. You have no right to be here. You have assaulted dimensions and walked into my court. That was very foolish."

The children of Horus chimed in in unison, "Very foolish."

Lucifer changed. His joking demeanour vanished and he stood before Ra looking dangerous. "You dared to send my son back to Earth. It was not for you to decide. He has something I want."

Ra walked around Lucifer with his hands behind his back. "I had every right, Lucifer. Thutmose was brought to me having being almost killed by you. He is Egyptian. He recognises Egyptian gods and came here to be weighed and measured. He was not found wanting, despite the fact you tried to blame him for a murder he did not commit, nor would ever have had the heart to commit. You, on the other hand, your putrid stink tells me all I need to know about you."

Lucifer began to rage, but he couldn't change.

"Oh, lost something, have we Lucifer? Or should I say… Luci? Something like, oh, I don't know, how about the ability to change into a dragon or a putrid demon? You stupid, stupid angel. It was dangerous for you to come to my court, thinking you could make demands and frighten me. This is MY court, Lucifer, and I command what happens here."

Ra walked around to the front of Lucifer. He looked at him with an anger that betrayed his ancient authority, an authority that had followed him over millennia. The children of Horus gathered around Ra and Maat released a feather. Lucifer could not move; he was frozen to the spot. Ra stretched out his hand and removed Lucifer's heart in one painless swoop. Lucifer's eyes widened. "You have been weighed." He placed Lucifer's heart on the scale with Maat's feather. The scales fell with a clang. "You have been measured." And looking into Lucifer's eyes, Ra said, "And you have definitely been found wanting." And at that, Lucifer fell to the floor.

Michael looked towards God.

"Oh no, what has he done now?" said God, rolling his eyes.

CHAPTER 25

Bastet had always promised herself that whatever happened, she would see Thutmose again. She had hardly thought about any other god since the first day she met him at the Cairo market. She had fought for him in the battle and she was pretty sure his debt to her would be paid. She knew exactly where he lived in Paris and intended to pay him a visit. She closed her eyes and when she opened them, there he was, asleep on his bed. She stood looking at him. He looked troubled, but she thought she could take that troubled look away. She walked over to his bedside. She quickly slipped into being a cat again; he had liked her when she was in Cairo and had told her she was beautiful. She jumped onto his bed and nudged his face. Thutmose moved his hand across his face. He was still sleeping. She nudged his face again and rubbed her face on his face. She put her nose on to the end of his nose.

Thutmose opened his eyes. He couldn't believe it. How did the cat get here? His veranda doors were open, perhaps she sprang up? "Well hello, little one," he laughed. "How did you get up here? Are you hungry or thirsty?" He picked her up and took her to his kitchen. He put her down on the floor. She purred and rubbed around his legs. He bent down and scuffed her ears. He put some milk in a bowl for her, but she ignored it. "Well, suit yourself," he said, "but I'm tired, I need to sleep." He walked back to his bedroom, closely followed by Bastet, and shut the door in her face. She changed immediately. Not quite the welcome she expected. She had another plan. She quietly opened the door and slipped back into cat mode and curled up next to him on the bed. She decided she would also go to sleep and then surprise him in the morning.

God was at a loss as to what to do. "I can't go to the court of Ra, Michael. It is not for me to enter there. Lucifer's kingdom is different. He is my son and between us all, we balance the laws of mankind. Egyptian law is different, they do things differently there. We need Lucifer back. It's true, but I really don't want to upset the laws of the universe. It could take years to put right."

"Thutmose should go," said Michael. God looked at Metatron, who nodded in agreement.

"Michael," God's voice became soft and compassionate, "if you want to fetch Lucifer, you can. I would stop time for you if I thought this would make you happy."

Michael smiled. "No, Father. From the bottom of my heart, I thank you, but I really think this would help both Thutmose and Lucifer."

"Then it shall be."

In the morning, Thutmose rose to find the most beautiful, dark-haired woman in his kitchen, wearing not much more than a chiffon Egyptian dress. The jewels and fastenings rustled when she walked. She turned and looked at him; her beautifully lined charcoal eyes smiled a knowing smile and her beautiful red lips peeled back to reveal the whitest of teeth.

Her front teeth seemed to be sharpened to a little point which made her look very sexy. She was, by all accounts Thutmose thought, magnificent. He suddenly became quite shy; he couldn't remember going out last night or bringing anyone home. He certainly had not done that for at least 20 years.

She looked at him, bending her head slightly. "Good morning, Thutmose, you've definitely not woken up with bed head."

He grinned and put his hand through his hair. "I'm er, I'm really sorry, but if I went out last night, I can drink too much, not that I think you shouldn't be here, this is a lovely surprise, but I'm afraid I may have forgotten your name, and I'm not sure what I may have told you."

She was suddenly very close to him, searching his face and lightly sniffing him. Thutmose suddenly had the realisation that she might smell his 'stench' and quickly stepped away, accidently putting his hand out and touching her.

"Oh, so sorry…" Bastet smiled. "Thutmose, don't be so defensive, I like your smell." He shot her a very surprised look. "I've slept with you all night, curled up right by your stomach. Do you think I would not have smelled your scent?"

"What did you say your name was?"

"I didn't," she said, "but you can call me hot…" Bastet grabbed Thutmose and gave him a kiss that nearly knocked him off his feet. When she released him, he couldn't resist her and she didn't leave until the evening, when Thutmose fell into a deep, peaceful slumber. Bastet changed herself back into a cat and quietly slipped away. Outside, she slipped through the dimension and within seconds was walking the streets of Cairo with her tail in the air. Her purr was louder than usual. "Wow, what a god," she giggled.

Michael sat on the fence of Thutmose's veranda and waited until the sun rose and he heard him move. He walked into Thutmose's kitchen, then Thutmose walked in behind him.

"Whoa… now… wait… just wait a minute…"

Michael looked at him, puzzled. "What?"

"Don't tell me… you… please say you didn't… I didn't… I mean… we haven't…"

"We haven't what?"

"We haven't… oh no. I thought it was a woman, please don't tell anyone… I haven't… for ages… I mean… Oh no." Thutmose sat on a stool with his hands covering his eyes.

Michael suddenly understood. "OOOHHH I see, well now…" Michael swaggered towards Thutmose, moving his hips… Thutmose groaned… Then Michael started to laugh, a laugh that was like a dozen bells ringing… It was infectious, and Thutmose started to laugh.

"So, it wasn't?"

"No, no, it really wasn't," said Michael.

"Phew," said Thutmose. "That was nearly another friendship down the drain."

"So, who was it?"

Thutmose looked at his hands and suddenly went quite quiet. "I don't know, but she was beautiful. Soft, caring, tender… mother material." Then, he stopped as he reflected on the previous evening.

Michael got a vision and knew it was Bastet but she had her finger to her lips. She didn't want Thutmose to know, but she smiled a beautiful smile. "Well, I'm sure you will see her again, or certainly someone like her… Life is quite strange, as you know."

CHAPTER 26

Thutmose and Michael sat chatting, about nothing in particular. Thutmose talked about books, the seventeenth century, his meeting with Alexander the Great, the French Revolution, but he knew that Michael wasn't here to listen to small talk. "I suppose you know all this anyway," said Thutmose.

"No, we aren't invasive, we don't follow you every day of your life. You have your guardian angel for that. But as you are a god, your angel won't be with you all the time, only when you needed them most."

Thutmose looked dejected. "What happened to my guardian angel when my father took me to the dark dimension?"

Michael stood up. "They wouldn't have known. Lucifer is the father of lies."

Thutmose looked at his hands, turning them over. "I hate him. He could have killed me."

"Well, not quite killed," said Michael. "You have to remember, you are more than mortal. It wasn't you he was trying to kill, he was trying to get the energy you possess. It would have left you comatose for a few millennia, if that. God would have intervened, I'm sure."

"Yes, God would have killed me instead."

Michael went quiet. It was pointless arguing. "I heard you

when you came back from your discussions with him. Had I gone off on the wrong track, he would have killed me."

Thutmose's eyes flashed red. "I'm sorry, when I'm upset I can't seem to stop it."

"Don't apologise for who you are, Thutmose. It wasn't your fault you were born to Lucifer, you just need to fight the inner demon, as it were."

"I'm tired though, Michael." Thutmose looked up. "I knew this wasn't just a normal visit. Actually, none of my visitors are normal these days."

With a brief smile, Michael sat back down. After a slight pause, he began.

"We have a problem. Your father went to see Ra. You know your father; he is arrogant, self-centred, selfish, stupid, idiotic, childish, peevish, evil, corrupt, a complete and total degenerate and always, always breaks the rules." Thutmose listened but said nothing. "Well, he's in Limbo."

Thutmose looked at Michael. "What?"

Michael shrugged his shoulders. "He's in Limbo."

"How?" Thutmose started laughing. He laughed and laughed.

Michael sat patiently waiting for him to stop. "If you've quite finished? In his stupidity, he went to pick a fight with Ra, in his own court. Everyone knows, and so does Lucifer, that the playing field becomes hazardously uneven when you slip dimensions to the Egyptian plane. Ra did not find Lucifer amusing, and Lucifer tried to scare him into his way of thinking by trying to metamorphose. Much like we cannot change in Lucifer's kingdom, he could not change in Ra's. He was therefore stuck. Ra pulled his heart out and he was found wanting. The problem is, we need him back. The walls of the dimensions are shaking because we have lost balance, but Ra won't give him up. This is very dangerous for us."

"You want me to fetch him back?"

Michael went quiet. "The balance needs to be redressed."

"I'll go."

"Thutmose, there is a cost."

"My life for his, I'll go. We've discussed this before, Michael. Everyone, no matter who they are, mortal or immortal, rich or poor, all have a purpose in life. We are all here for a purpose, and this is mine. I'll go. I know I could take his job, but you know me, our father knows me. I'd be useless, I'd forgive everyone for everything… It's OK, I'll go."

Michael sighed, but he was glad that Thutmose had made the decision. The end of mankind had not been forecast for another five hundred years. This would stop it happening sooner.

"How do I get there?"

Michael held his hands above Thutmose's head and opened a portal. He shot straight up and disappeared out of sight. "Good luck," Michael whispered.

Thutmose found himself in the court of Ra. It was empty. "Hello, hello?" He walked around trying to find someone. "Ra, Your Majesty, Maat, Bru, are you here?"

Maat walked out of the brightness. She communicated with her mind. "Thutmose, you do not need to shout, we can hear you. You should not be here. Why have you come?"

"My father, I've come to take my father home."

Maat walked slowly to him. "I'm sorry, Thutmose, you cannot take him from here. He is in Limbo now. He will spend a thousand years there paying for his sins, at the end of which he will be weighed and measured again. We cannot let him go now."

"You don't understand. The dimensional walls are shaking, the world is out of balance, it could destroy the universe."

Maat looked sad. "I'm sorry, Thutmose, but it's too late, you have to leave now."

"No."

Maat looked confused. "Thutmose, you must leave."

"No, I'm not leaving without my father."

From the brightness emerged Horus' children. "Thutmose, you have been weighed and measured, you are a pure soul, you must leave before Ra returns."

Then there was a shake, and Ra stepped back into his court. He did not look pleased. "What is it with your family? This is my court, but for some reason, you and your father think you can step in and out of it. I am now going to give you the chance to step out of it."

"No, I came for my father. The dimensions are thinning, the balance must be redressed."

Ra closed his eyes. "Thutmose, I am asking you to leave. If you do not, I will destroy you. I will destroy your soul and nothing of you will remain."

Thutmose stepped forward. "Do it then, but your anger will not be justified and all the dimensions will be dangerously unstable. You told me that if you were in grave danger and there was someone who you could have with you, it would be me. Well, my father needs me; I am here to set him free. I give my life for his."

Ra looked into Thutmose's eyes. He had spoken the words that Ra really did not want to hear. He bowed his head, his eyes teared and the children of Horus moaned in pain.

"Thutmose, you have said the words I was hoping I would not hear; you have contracted with me. You have given me your very life and soul in return for the life and soul of another. I, Ra, cannot refuse."

Maat wept, that a soul so beautiful as Thutmose's should be removed to Limbo. "I will bring your father. You will have time to say goodbye."

Thutmose held up his head through the brightness. Lucifer returned. There was no one around; Ra, Maat and the children of Horus had disappeared.

"Well, about bloody time. What took you so long?"

Thutmose smiled. "Hello, Father."

"Well, come on then, let's get out of this place."

"I can't come with you, Father."

Lucifer stopped. "Oh don't start, Thutmose, what is it you want? I'll give you anything you want."

"I don't want anything, I just want the balance to be redressed, but for that to happen, I have to stay here."

Lucifer looked at Thutmose. He shook his wings, clearly trying to detract from the conversation. "Go, Father, it's fine, I love you, just go."

Lucifer stopped. "What's happened?"

"It doesn't matter, just go. I'll see you soon."

"You're lying. I'm the king of lies and you are lying to me. Maybe I'll teach you something good yet."

Thutmose smiled. He held out his hand. "Goodbye, Father."

Lucifer stretched out his hand, but it passed through Thutmose's. "Ra, Ra! Get bloody out here now!" shouted Lucifer.

"Father please, you don't need to shout. They can hear

your mind. Please, don't cause any further trouble."

Lucifer looked at the floor. "It's too white here, too white. At least where I live we have lots of different colours. Can't you just run for it? It might be different when we get outside."

Thutmose said nothing.

"You never were much of a talker. Why? Why, Thutmose? I tried to kill you and you have given your life for me."

"Mankind needs balance, Father. It has to be redressed. Good and Evil will always exist on Earth. Both sides need to be taken care of, and you are the best at your job."

Lucifer smiled. "Ask me anything. I'll answer anything you want me to."

"Well, not that it matters now, but how would I give up my immortal life on Earth to find peace and an end to the days I have spent? I never wanted immortality."

Lucifer put his head on his side. "You fall asleep and wish. You wish like you have never wished before. You start at the very beginning of your memories and when you come to the first memory that makes you sad, you wish, then you sleep, then it's over."

Thutmose smiled. "Liar."

Lucifer expanded his wings and stretched. The gold and colours shot through him like rays of sun; his golden breastplate lit up the court of Ra; his light shone so blindingly that Thutmose could hardly see him. His eyes lit up and shone like fluorescent pearl and he looked incredibly beautiful. His hair flowed and his smile was full of warmth and compassion. "No, Thutmose, I really am not lying. We are in the court of Ra and though I hate it, I cannot lie in the court of Ra. You are my son and I promised to answer your question. I have answered you truthfully. When you are lonely in that pit of despair, close your eyes and do what I say. You will sleep for a thousand years."

Thutmose could not believe his eyes. "Father, you are magnificent."

Lucifer put his hand out to Thutmose's cheek and touched it. The scar Thutmose had carried all his life was removed and his beauty shone as fine as Lucifer's. Tears began to flow down Lucifers face. "Thutmose, I am truly sorry for the life that you have led. You have become the person I would have wanted to be had I grown up mortal. You are a credit to me and your mother and for that night, I did truly love your mother. You were made of love, Thutmose, and that is why you have never crossed over to my side. My father has forsaken me, and that is my fault, but I will not forsake you. Thutmose, you will always be blessed by angels and you will see the light of day again, I promise you. Now sleep, my son, and know that you will be forever in my heart."

Thutmose closed his eyes and fell asleep. The court of Ra disappeared and Lucifer found himself back in Hell. Lucifer shouted up to God.

God heard his voice and turned around. "Lucifer."

"Father, get him back."

"He took your place, Lucifer. He had a choice. The world is on balance and we cannot disturb it again. I have too much respect for Ra."

"Father, get him back."

"Or what, Lucifer?"

Lucifer couldn't think of anything. "He is my son, Father, he is therefore your son. Please do not let him pay for my mistakes."

God looked at Lucifer. "Lucifer, this is not my fight. He is by all accounts Egyptian. You need the council of the Egyptian gods; they are your only hope. He is out of my jurisdiction now."

Lucifer turned on his heel and flew fast towards Abu Simbel. He suddenly felt emotions and as he looked to his right, he saw Michael, Jophiel, Metatron, Raguel, Ariel, Uriel, Raphael, Sandalphon, Gabriel, Azrael, Chamuel, Zadkiel, Raziel, Jeremiel; they were all going with him. He was not forsaken by his brothers, at least not today.

Spiritual communication had cut through time and space and as they landed in Abu Simbel, they were met by Geb, Bastet, Seth, Isis, Osiris, Thoth, Sekhmet, Sokar and Wadjet. When they had gathered, Lucifer stepped forward. Everyone fell quiet. "I want my son back. Thutmose has the soul of an angel and doesn't belong in Limbo."

Thoth looked around at everyone. "You will be meeting the council, Lucifer, and you will need a hell of a good reason to let them release Thutmose from Limbo, and who will be replacing him?"

Lucifer looked at the other angels. "No one."

"What?"

"No one. We have come to take him home."

"Impossible," said Sokar. "If someone leaves Limbo, you have to replace them, you know this."

"I'll try and talk them round," said Lucifer. "I know, as soon as we enter that hall, we will be impotent of our powers. We have nothing. I don't want to fight, I just want my son."

"Lucifer, this is really dangerous," said Thoth.

"Then why are you all here? Your immortal souls are in danger."

"Because, danger is our name and escaping is our game," said Jophiel. Everyone looked at Jophiel and his quip broke the tension; they all laughed.

"We need a plan," said Sandalphon.

"And a drink," laughed Jophiel.

A portal with a golden light suddenly shone from the entrance of Abu Simbel. "We're on, they are expecting us," nodded Osiris, and as they all entered, the portal shut down.

Ra was sitting in his throne. "Lucifer, this is getting very tedious. I have done you one favour. You are mistaken to come and seek another."

"I seek the council."

Ra surveyed everyone Lucifer had brought with him. "You bring gods and angels, Lucifer, are you seeking the council of war?"

Lucifer moved forward. "I seek the council. You weighed my heart and said I was found wanting. I am trying to redress the balance."

Ra stood up and faced Lucifer. "Redress the balance? You have already redressed it, Lucifer, your son has taken your place. You do not need to seek the council, there is nothing further to say." Thoth walked forward. "Thoth, have you come to scribe for me?"

"Ra, I have come to support a father who has lost his son. I request that you, as one of the mightiest of the mighty, call the council and let him present his case. Time is nothing to any of us, and if it takes a thousand years, we still have lost nothing."

"If it takes a thousand years, Thutmose will be free," said Jophiel.

Michael looked at Jophiel and whispered, "Shut up, Joph,

he's making our case."

"Thoth, one of your talents is the Law, so we will need our best council."

"Law?" whispered Raguel to Michael.

"Yes, he was the maker of Law."

"Great."

Smiles and nods could be seen through the group. Ra looked at Lucifer and kept looking; his eyes pierced through him and Lucifer felt dizzy, then Ra abruptly looked away. "Alright, let's waste a few more thousand years." There was a loud sound like wind in a tunnel and the children of Horus appeared before a council of six.

CHAPTER 27

THE FINALE

Ahead of the council was Hathor, then Amun, followed by Anubis, Atum, Shu and to the shock of the group, Seth. Seth smirked as he walked past Lucifer.

"Oh, bugger," whispered Lucifer.

Geb tutted. "I cannot believe bloody Shu is on the council. Now I can see him, I could just thump him one."

"No you won't," said Thoth. "I've got enough to fight about as it is." Geb folded his arms and gave Shu a very hard stare. Thoth was looking at Anubis and they seemed to be communicating. "We may have a supporter," said Thoth to Lucifer and patted his shoulder. "Try and keep it together, Lucifer. Don't lose your temper, it could put us at a disadvantage."

"Why does everyone think I'm going to be the problem?" Lucifer frowned.

The angels looked at each other, all shrugging. "Don't know, Lucifer, it's not like you to lose your temper, is it?"

Michael looked at Lucifer. "Lucifer, it will be fine," he said, "you'll see." Lucifer wanted to speak with Michael, but just for once, he knew this was neither the place nor the time.

"Court is in session!" shouted Maat. A small giggle rang around the court, then it stopped. They all suddenly realised that this was usual.

Thoth stepped forward. "We are here to plead the case for Lucifer's son, Thutmose. He is in Limbo for a thousand years having saved his father to keep balance in the universe."

Seth let out a loud, "Humph."

"Do you have something to say, Seth?" said Ra.

"No, nothing, other than he was trying to kill his own son and killed mine instead."

"Well at least you got that right," snapped Lucifer.

Thoth looked at Lucifer with a 'keep it quiet' face. He continued, "We want to retrieve Thutmose because he never wanted to be a god. This is obvious. He has taken the opportunity to forfeit his immortality to save his father and redress the balance of mankind, which is at risk. I do not need to remind you that had he not done so, there would have been a domino effect which would have collapsed all the dimensions eventually, and we would all have been in great danger, if not finished completely. We all owe our lives to him, but can I just add, that if Ra hadn't taken Lucifer's heart in the first place, then the dimensions would not have shaken and we wouldn't be here now."

The court was quiet. Ra leaned on his elbow and began to rub the side of his face.

"My suggestion is that Thutmose is released from Limbo and returned to his own time to be able to continue on in a life that he sees fit, with no interference from any of us. He could not help that he is Lucifer's son, and when he dies, at such time that God sees fit, then he will be called to redress any and all of his shortcomings in his human lifetime and a decision will be made to despatch his soul to where it should end its eternity. Whether that be Heaven or Hell should not be decided by us. Any and all energy should be removed and disposed of sensibly."

The council talked amongst themselves and Atum addressed the room. "We hear your argument, Thoth, but if we remove Thutmose, then we will need a replacement. Do any of you here volunteer yourselves?"

Michael moved a foot and Sandalphon pulled him back. "No, Michael."

Atum smiled. "We have no doubt that Thutmose was, or is, a great warrior for the cause, but as was pointed out, and as we all know, Lucifer tried to kill him for his own benefit. Thutmose is currently asleep. A thousand years will fly by for him and when he wakes, we can consider what to do with him then. Do you not agree?" Seth sat nodding his head and staring at Lucifer who was getting more aggravated as the seconds passed.

Jophiel tapped Lucifer on the shoulder. "Lucifer, stop staring, it will make you worse." They were all sitting, but levitating, and Lucifer's legs were crossed but his right leg was flicking front to back very quickly. Lucifer wished he could dragon and tear through the dimensions to free Thutmose.

"OOOOOO, I think not!" shouted Seth. "You're impotent here, Lucifer. Fancy that… impotent."

Lucifer stood up and Ariel pulled him back down. Seth smirked at the effect it was having on Lucifer. Lucifer folded his arms and was rocking backwards and forwards. Gabriel moved and sat with him. "Lucifer, please, calm down… How's your skateboarding going?" Lucifer looked at Gabriel like he was going to eat her. "Just asking."

Thoth carried on. "There are plenty of people who could take Thutmose's place. It does not have to be a god; there are many humans who have not had a worthy life."

"Yes, but it is rather a novelty to have a god in Limbo, whether he's sleeping or not," reflected Ra. The argument for release seemed to be faltering.

"It's because it's me, isn't it?" said Lucifer, through gritted teeth. "If it was anyone else in this dimension, then everyone would be in everyone else's chariot, but no, it's Lucifer, the bad boy, let's make him miserable for the rest of eternity. None of you like me, none of you love me. I've always been on the outside."

Seth started to play an invisible violin, except there was music playing…

"Right, that's it," said Lucifer. "You're dead…"

"Oh, not this again," moaned Seth.

Lucifer saw red and ploughed forward at speed, grabbing Seth by the neck, and before you could say 'eternal life' the whole court was in an uproar. It took all the angels to pull Lucifer off Seth, who was laughing so much, when Lucifer let go, he could hardly sit upright on his seat.

Maat was shouting for order and Shu made himself invisible to avoid being hit by Geb who was trying to take advantage of the fray. Everyone was shouting at everyone else until they heard a voice that shocked them into quietness.

"I'll do it, I'll take his place, just please, stop fighting. This isn't who Thutmose is." They all turned and there stood Bruharis. "I'll do it, I'll redress the balance."

Seth, although a god, looked drained of colour. It was Lucifer's turn to start laughing.

Raguel looked at Lucifer. "Dude, not cool…"

"Sorry," he said, but kept tittering anyway.

Seth walked to Bruharis. "Bru, you cannot do this."

"Yes Father, I can. I will be giving back what YOU took away from hundreds of families in our village. Have you any idea how much sorrow and heartache it caused? I know you were trying to save me, but I still had to leave the village. All those children who grew up without fathers. This is my redemption, if I take over from Thutmose. It will only be for a thousand years, and I think I am due a break. What do you say, Ra?"

The court changed from a bright gold to dark stone. Ra walked to Bruharis. "Bru, we have weighed and measured you, you were not found wanting. Thutmose and you are made of all that is good is in the world, despite who your fathers were. Your offer is too much. We cannot allow you to cover for Thutmose; it is not allowed."

"Then change the rules. Times are changing, Ra, life is changing. Change the rules."

"Bru, our rules are what has held our dimension together for millennia. If we change them now, anything could happen."

"He's my brother, my heart." Bru thumped his chest with his fist. "We know each other. If you keep him in there, you may as well be keeping me." Bru put his head down. "Ra, you are without doubt the majesty of all gods, but I am begging you, as your servant, please, let my brother go. I can do a thousand years. Really, I can, it's a breeze. I've already done a few."

"NO!" shouted Seth. "I will not allow it."

Ra and Bruharis looked at Seth. "It's not your decision, Dad." Bruharis turned back to Ra.

Ra placed his hand on Bruharis' shoulder. "The council will retire; we will make our decision."

EPILOGUE

Thutmose sat looking at the constellations in the sky. He knew all of them. He wondered if he were human again, would he remember them all? Would he care? Would he be able to count them and know which universe revolved around which universe? He saw shooting stars in the sky and supposed it was the angels taking their places with humans around the world, comforting them, teaching them to be good and helping them in their hour of need. His had been a long and strange immortal life. He wasn't sure if he would ever believe it if someone had told him it had happened.

God had told him that he had choices. He could remain a god and stay immortal until the world finally became cold again and everything died, ready for when God would start his plan again. He could work with his father, but Lucifer wasn't happy about that choice. Suppose he tried to overthrow him? Or God had offered to reset time. Now that was huge, but he really liked Thutmose and wanted what was best for him. Thutmose had always wanted to get married and have children, but then he would get old and die, and would anyone remember him one hundred years from now?

Thutmose felt a small draft, but he didn't need to look to see who it was. "Hello, Mother."

"Hello, Thutty."

He smiled. "I'm trying to make my decision."

She sat on the sand with him. It made him smile because she sort of sank into it but didn't get dusty. "I know, I heard you."

"Do you have any suggestions?"

She laid her hand on his hand. "I think whatever decision your heart makes, will be the right one."

"That's a crafty get out."

"Yes, but here's the thing, I am not you. My decisions are not your decisions, and besides, whatever I said, you'd probably do the opposite. You're my son and I love you, but I'm not going to help you make your decision."

He looked up at the night sky. "I can see Achilles."

She looked at the constellation and looked at Thutmose. "The story of Achilles is similar to yours; he was given an option of staying with his mother and meeting a beautiful girl and getting married, or going to Troy. He went to Troy and died, but we all know who Achilles is. He's a bit arrogant though."

"You know Achilles?"

"I don't know him; he was at a party I went to. He was there with Patroclus and was showing off. Bit confused, but he has eternity to work himself out."

"Parties? They have parties? Do you ever see my father, I mean my real father?"

"I've seen him once. He's more together now. He understands that what happened wasn't my fault and he loves you. He is sorry and embarrassed about how he treated you. He can't see you yet, but maybe he will one day."

"Maybe."

They chatted for a while, and when the stars started to go out, she looked towards the horizon. "I need to go. I love you, Thutmose, I always will. Please… make your decision carefully. Don't rush into anything." She stroked his face and was gone.

Thutmose returned to look at the night sky as it faded and a beautiful dawn began to take its place. *Nice going, our father,* he thought. God heard him and smiled. He thought about Achilles; he thought about Ra riding his golden chariot across the sky. He lay back with his hands behind his head and remembered being in Limbo. He remembered all those people who were walking around, not aware that there were others there too. He knew, because he was a god, but none of the people spoke to each other or conversed with each other, they were effectively alone for the next one thousand years. They needed a champion, someone to fight for them and hear their cases again. The world was changing, but would Ra?

He knew he didn't have much time; the sun would be rising soon and God had given him until sunrise to make his decision. "Are you ready for a drink before decision time?"

He looked up. "Yes, Bru, I think I am."

"Great. Which century? Which country?"

THE END

ABOUT THE AUTHOR

M.J. Heywood was born in Staffordshire. She has a BA (Hons) and M.A. in Classical Studies from the Open University. She wrote her debut novel after writing drafts of bits of stories for two years. She lives in Newcastle-under-Lyme with her husband and her beautiful cat Misty. When she isn't writing, she is interviewing people on her radio station MHLive or playing her cello and learning to play the guitar (badly).